— THE RETURN TO THE —
LOST EL DORADO

W. MICHAEL GAZDAR, D.C.

W. MICHAEL GAZDAR, D.C.
Walnut Creek, California

Published and distributed by: JMCC
First Edition: 2020

2021 Ygnacio Valley Road, Suite C-204
Walnut Creek, California 94598
Phone: (925) 939-2225
Fax: (925) 939-8017

Email: michael@gazdar.com
Web: www.michaelgazdar.com

This book is a work of fiction. Names, characters, places and incidents are products of the author's imagination, and are used factitiously. Any resemblance to actual events, local people or persons living or dead is entirely coincidental.

Library of Congress Catalogue Number: 2020919335
Gazdar, Michael

THE RETURN TO THE LOST EL DORADO

ISBN (e book): 978-0-9645301-2-6

ISBN (Trade Paperback): 978-0-9645301-3-3

Printed in the United States of America

ACKNOWLEDGMENTS

No one writes a book alone. I would like to take this opportunity to thank the people who have helped me along the way.

Cover design by: The Unique Book Cover

Back Cover Photo by: CBJ Gazdar

Formatting by: Nicole Hayley Art

Copyeditor: Linda Jay

Technical Assistance: Michael Wells

Beta Reader: Janet Baillie

Publishing Assistance: Eric V. Van Der Hope

Website/Media: Tim Grahl

DEDICATION

This book is dedicated to my wife, Teri and our three children, Christian, Brandon, and Jonathan

Dad loves you guys more than you will ever know.

CONTENTS

CONTENTS

PROLOGUE

THE SMALL BROWN-SKINNED WOMAN from the Amazon raised her arms up to the full moon, as though imploring it to change the course of nature, by bending it to do her will. She looked no more than twenty years of age, but was really much older. Her blue eyes were wide-open and she chanted an ancient ritual of death. Alone, in this part of the jungle, next to a hidden tributary, that eventually found its way to the mighty Amazon, nothing came near her. Neither man, nor beast. Although the deadly snakes, panthers and caiman were near, they instinctively gave her a wide berth.

Dressed only in a loincloth, with a heavy beaded necklace that covered her chest, and a native headdress made of coconut, beads and feathers, she suddenly screamed to the Heavens.

"Voodoo rites! Female native daughter of the rich woman! Servant of Satan! The Chibchas who are confused and are about to ruin everything! Send me the man named Thomas! Together we will curse the child called Damien, son of the betrayers of the Chibchas and defiler of this land. Bring back the holy piranha with their evil hearts and giant smiles.

"To you Bill Treese. You have defiled my mother. I will curse you as well!" She spat on the ground, then began to cut her hand with a large knife, which had hung from her belt. Her blood dropped onto her spit, suddenly beginning to bubble and churn. Mysteriously, the liquid began to double and triple in volume, even though she had stopped bleeding herself.

She took a large bamboo staff with a shrunken head mounted on top, and began to draw ancient symbols in the liquid, which by now was making rivulets in the mud. Suddenly, rain began to fall, as the dark clouds above began swirling and collapsing upon themselves. Thunder rolled in her direction, propelled by heavy winds.

"Demon, exorcist of the Amazon! You are now entering the deepest hole in all of the Amazon; now it descends on you!" she screamed into the wind. "Your Cross and Cloak will not spite my magic. They will do you no good. Either I will possess these souls or you and your tribe will be laid waste! Hear me Lucifer. Take them now and release the winds and the fish again!"

Suddenly, as if by magic, the water before her began to boil. Shapes started rising up from this deep part of the river, which began churning madly, as the snouts of the giant piranha, some over 15 feet long, appeared and the fish began circling. As the thunder rolled, and the water churned, the piranha began to pick up speed, circling faster and faster. The water seemed to rise above the bank and stay, held, there as if by a giant glass retainer.

Her eyes rolled back into her head and, as impossible as it

seemed, she began to levitate above the ground. Bent backwards as if possessed, her body began to hover over the center of the circle of piranha. Seemingly immune to the wind and the fury of the waves, she floated there, while being pummeled by the froth and fury of the waves.

A low guttural sound that escaped from her lips, rose and fell eerily, then began to gain momentum.

Everything was coming to a crescendo. Her moans reached a fevered pitch as the wind howled and thunder crashed.

"La Diablia! La Diabiloc!" she shouted.

Suddenly a bolt of lightning came down and struck her! It seemed to pass through her, turning her body translucent and she was hurled onto the shore. The wind died down almost instantly, and the clouds began to clear. The full moon, which had been hidden by the sudden formation of the clouds, appeared again. The giant piranha were gone. The woman lay on the ground, panting. Her loincloth, necklace and headdress had been torn off and she was naked. The wind had died down and there was total silence.

As she looked up at the moon, she smiled.

CHAPTER ONE

THE BEGINNINGS

BILL TREESE LEANED OVER THE forward Bulkhead of the PT 109 and stared into the gigantic black hole in the water. There were secrets in that hole. Secretes that spanned centuries. It was up to him to find out what lay beneath him in these waters.

He stood up and shook his head, then looked around at the rest of the nearby Caribbean Islands that dotted the horizon. Not less than twenty islands were in sight. So why was this black hole here, by itself, in the turquoise water of the Southern Caribbean?

It was 11:30 A.M.; the sun was about to hit its zenith. It was even hot on the water. It was over 100 degrees most of the time, and it didn't let up.

Bill grabbed a towel off the foredeck and wiped the sweat off his brow and the back of his neck. "Jonas," he called to one of the Brazilian divers, "*Como esta?* Are you ready to dive?"

"*Si Capitán.*"

"What about Miguel?"

"*Si Capitán.* He too is geared up and ready to descend."

"What about Carlos?"

"*Si, Capitán,* he knows how to keep the boat steady, and then maneuver when he has to."

Bill took another look overboard into the black hole and shuddered. In spite of the heat, which became oppressive at times, a chill, which went down his spine. He made a quick decision.

"Carlos, you are on deck and at the helm. I'm going to dive down with Julian and Miguel."

"*Si, Capitán.* It is your boat and your charter."

Julian Jonas, a young man of 22, with a strong body and spiked hair, like American TV actors, looked at his *compadre* with an impassive face. He was wary of this deep hole in the sea. While Julian was comfortable doing deep dives on wrecks and reefs, this abyss was deep, uncharted and unrecorded. This area of South America was known locally as the Devil's Triangle of South America, where ships, planes and men disappear on a regular basis.

Julian sighed. He would follow his boss, diving deep into the ocean to see what they could find.

Bill had already set up a line of air tanks halfway as deep as the hole, which was an estimated 500 feet down. These were set up as decompression stops to help them dive safely and to prevent them from absorbing too much nitrogen, which could result in decompression sickness, otherwise known as the bends. This was a situation where the nitrogen in his blood would expand and cause his capillaries to erupt and explode, leading to a very painful death.

The problem was that after going 200 feet down a diver was

in danger of nitrogen narcosis, which meant that he or she could become disorganized while down there and, not only become confused, but also lose consciousness and die.

Bill, Julian and Miguel finished gearing up, wearing the best equipment they could muster for a deep dive. Bill had been doing this type of diving for over 30 years. Both Julian and Miguel, raised on the Amazon River in Brazil were more than expert divers. Each of the men had free dived, meaning without tanks for over 100 feet.

Bill was optimistic that they could dive at least 175 feet, by breathing shallowly for several minutes. They would try to go beyond that depth, but would have to use their diving tables, depending on how long they stayed down, and stopping and decompressing at each dive tank. This process would take a while.

But for sure, there was treasure in that hole. This dive was no fluke.

The plan was that Julian and Miguel would descend first to 75 feet and then signal all clear. Bill would then descend to that depth and then the two other divers would descend at 25' intervals, with each one trailing the other in a "hop scotch" pattern, designed to maximize their view of the descent. They would then turn around 360 degrees, searching with powerful flashlights designed to penetrate the darkest depths of the hole.

Julian and Miguel sat on the outer railings of the PT 109. Quietly they both tilted backwards, holding their face-masks, until they tumbled over backwards into the waters below. Bill, his face filled with concern, scanned the horizon with care. He would wait five minutes and then descend. An underwater screech horn was set in place in case they had to scuttle the dive.

Bill looked at his watch. It had reached the 4.25-minute mark. He sat on the rail, ready to fall backwards into the warm Caribbean waters.

Suddenly Carlos appeared on deck. "*Capitán* Bill!" he shouted. "Contact from Colombia. They say it is urgent they talk to you!"

Bill blinked rapidly. His morning coffee, began to churn in his stomach. "OK. Thanks." He stood up stiffly and dropped his tanks and buoyancy-controlled vest, then bent over and kicked off his fins and weight belt. Quickly he went to the radio room, knowing that the divers down below were waiting for him.

Bill grabbed the microphone and headset. After about 30 seconds he said, "Ok. I got it."

He swung out of the radio room and back up on deck. "Carlos!" he yelled sharply. "Set off the underwater alarm! Bring them up. No more diving today."

Carlos looked at him with surprise and confusion.

Bill simply looked at him and gestured emphatically that was what he wanted him to do. Carlos nodded in affirmation and walked toward the stern. He reached down and triggered the underwater blast, which meant that the divers below needed to come to the surface as quickly as possible.

Once they came aboard, they would hoist up the diving lines and the air tanks. Bill watched as Carlos, steadied the boat, moved into position to receive the divers and then brought them onboard with no problems.

The two divers surfaced and came aboard, offloading their scuba gear. They looked at Bill, who was now looking at navigational charts, expecting an explanation. In rapid fire Spanish the others spoke to Carlos demanding an answer as to why the dive had been stopped.

"*Quien sabe?*" Who knows?" was all Carlos could tell them.

"Julian!" Bill said sharply. "Plot a course for us to get back to the Amazon as quickly as possible. We can't enter the mouth as it would be too risky, so find us a tributary that is calm, where we can circumvent the mouth and head upstream past the heavy torrents."

"Aye, *Capitán*. But why? Where are we going?"

"Back to Brazil and maybe to Colombia. Thomas Reichen has escaped prison."

****

Professor John Waales looked up at the burning torch lighting the dark tunnel, deep in the bowels of the Lost El Dorado mine. That light was a bright reflection temporarily brightening his mind as much or more than it did the dark tunnel following the thin line of gold. A string of fluorescent lights was stretched across the rock ceiling, which emitted a soft glow, leading from the entrance to where John was working. Not enough light for exploring, but just enough to find your way in and out of the tunnel.

John stood up and wiped the sweat off his brow. He was alone in this cavern. The ore was about to run out, and he was trying to find the vein that would be an offshoot to this line of gold. It was expected that this line, which led deep into the rock, and, truth be told, would actually go deep, under the Mighty Amazon River itself, would lead directly to the mother lode. This hope would dwarf the already extremely valuable and enormous volume of gold in the current village-"The Village of Gold!"

John knew that time was of the essence. There were two

reasons for this. First, this mine was new and had barely been explored. No safety structures had been built and there were no structural supports; the cave could cave in at any time and no rescuers would arrive. John would simply die in his continuing quest for the gold. The second reason, was, in the past year that he had been here in the Amazon, researching and mining gold, John realized that the natives had been becoming increasingly unhappy with his presence. They wanted him to leave, so they could return to their normal lives.

At first, after he and his friends had helped them reclaim their long-lost village from their evil cousins, the native Chibchas had been only too happy to help him research and explore the lost Amazon village gold mines. They were able to take out an amount of gold, which helped to finance their quest and rescue. They natives even allowed John and his colleagues to explore further and take out a small percentage more of gold, as long as it was divided with them.

But he knew his days here, mining for gold, were numbered.

John Waales picked up his pick and began to tap near the currently exposed vein. He saw that the gold tracings extended far beyond where he had expected them to stop. For another 30 minutes he worked hard under the hot torch light, with little fresh air and lots of dust. He coughed harshly for a minute. His eyes were watering and he wiped them on his shirt. He stepped back and shown his powerful flashlight down the cavern. The tracings of gold were getting smaller and within about 10 feet disappeared completely. He focused his light on a dark spot of gold three feet behind him. It was small, dark and complex. It looked different, and by his calculation, headed immediately toward the river. So, he had been running parallel to the river, which was approximately 20-40 feet away.

John went to the unusual spot and tapped his pick above and below the fault. A large chunk of ore fell out onto the ground below. John picked it up. It was heavy and looked like pure gold. He pointed his flashlight up the fissure, which widened and then went deep into the wall. He didn't see the crack that had formed in the rock wall, above the gold he had just extracted that was marching its way to the top of the tunnel and then back towards the direction of the entrance

John stepped back and checked his watch. To his surprise, it was after midnight! He still had to leave the tunnel, which would take him almost an hour, and then another hour trek through the jungle, back to the village. The jungle path was relatively safe and partially lit. Nonetheless, it was still the jungle. He decided to smear some mud over the wall, rather than leave it exposed. He dropped the gold nugget into his pants pocket.

As he started to turn around, he felt it first before he heard it. The ground started shaking, slowly at first, then with more force. A deep rumbling crashing sounded behind him. Suddenly it seemed as if the walls and ceiling were coming down all around him. Instinctively, he dove forward, under a three-foot-high natural archway in the rock wall. The last thing he was conscious of before a rock hit him in the back of the head was, the realization that he had, in fact, stayed in the tunnel too long.

Then he lost consciousness.

****

Thomas Reichen's eyes squinted into the light of the early dawn, while looking over the Amazon River, near its mouth, which produced a flow of over eight trillion gallons of water per day. As he was lying on his stomach in the dense foliage of the jungle that fronted the river, he looked around and took inventory of his body's condition and his situation.

His escape from the temporary prison he was locked in wasn't pretty. *But what escape ever is?* he asked himself. At least he didn't have to hide in a sewer system, or dig down several feet into the slimy earth. He didn't have to vault over an electric fence surrounded by barbed wire, and he didn't have to be loaded into the back of a garbage truck, next to moldy food and shitty sheets.

He simply removed the clip from the ballpoint pen used by the Brazilian police officer who had booked him and placed it into his mouth when no one was looking. He kept the clip lodged in his cheek for 48 hours, which was no small feat, since he was exhausted from his travels from up the Amazon while he was a prisoner on Bill Treese's PT boat.

Eventually, as the situation, and also the guards settled down in front of the new "guest," it became easier to gain their trust. More importantly, they relaxed. First, Terragon, the new guard, allowed him to be released from his shackles whenever he was inside the small cell. After all, where could he go? He was stuck there behind bars.

Then Freddy, the more experienced and also the greedier guard, told Thomas, for a few dollars he kept hidden in his clothes, when the guards would be on "skeleton detail,"- meaning, only one guard would be between his cell and the outside wall. He told Thomas it was also likely that the guard would be sleeping while on-duty from 2-4 AM.

Thomas simply had to pick the lock and quietly make his way to the guard, relieve him of his keys and slip out the side gate of the prison.

In fact, it all went well. Up to a point.

When Thomas reached the side gate, which was, unfortunately, bathed in light, the tower guards immediately saw him.

Suddenly, the escape alarm sounded and the tower guards opened fire. As the bullets rained down, Thomas was able to open the gate and slip outside the prison wall. The bad news was that he had taken two superficial hits, one to the fleshy part of his right thigh, and one to his left buttock. Neither wound was serious, but both hurt like hell.

Suddenly, in Spanish, someone yelled, "Release the dogs!" Thomas froze and waited, listening. He heard a crash as the inside kennel was opened. The dogs were loose and barking in protest. They rushed the gates, not too far from Thomas, and howled in frustration as the heavy outer gates kept them back.

He waited. He heard a shout in Spanish; "Open the outer kennels!"

His heart sank. The guards would find him in a minute. Then, if he wasn't torn to bits by the dogs, he would be dragged back to his cell by the guards, probably missing an arm or a leg.

Suddenly, he heard loud voices yelling in rapid-fire Spanish. From what he could discern, it sounded like the outside kennels had failed to open! He pushed himself up and looked toward the compound. The outside dogs, were still in their pens, and were howling in protest. Some threw themselves against the iron gates, but to no avail.

Thomas knew that was a good sign. The dogs would be held back and he could escape. He looked down. A sigh of relief escaped him as calm flooded his body.

Suddenly, loud voices came from the outside kennels. One dog, Fritze the dominant German shepherd, 10 years old and 120 pounds, had managed to escape though a part of the gate that was partially blocked by the opening mechanism. Alone, Fritze charged forward, paying no heed to his handlers, who we left behind.

Thomas heard the barking and jumped up. He ran to the river and waded in, hoping to throw off the dog's scent. Then he saw Fritze in the jungle and heard him crying for the chase. Thomas splashed down the river and finally pulled up into a grove of fern trees. He waited, holding his breath, as he heard the dog racing behind him.

As Fritze ran past him, Thomas relaxed for a moment. Suddenly, the dog was standing right front of him, his lips foaming and his jaw chomping. Thomas' hands flew reflexively up to the dog's throat and grabbed him mercilessly. He squeezed his throat until the dog cried out. Thomas clenched him tightly for a minute, then hurled him into the river. The half-conscious dog, began to tread water, moving slowly toward the shore.

Thomas seized the moment. He leapt to his feet and ran the length of the river toward the jungle and away from the lights of the city. He knew exactly where he was going. There was a pilot in the jungle he could trust, to get him out of here, fast. He had a score to settle, and a fortune to make, but first, he needed to see Charley.

****

Bill Treese sat at the controls of his WWII Patrol Torpedo boat, the PT 109. It was a symbolic number, as the original PT 109 was captained by John F. Kennedy in the South Pacific in 1942, and was sunk after being rammed by a Japanese destroyer.

It was close to midnight as Bill piloted past the Caribbean Ocean, to the Atlantic, Ocean, heading back to Colombia and the Amazon River.

Bill didn't smoke anymore, but if he did, he knew he would take a long drag on an unfiltered Camel cigarette right now just to clear his head.

His former prisoner Thomas Reichen had escaped. After the events at the Village of the Lost El Dorado, and the subsequent arrest and detainment of Mr. Reichen, who had led the revolt, Treese had locked Reichen in chains below deck. Treese had transported him all the way to Brazil from the Colombia region of the Amazon.

So, Bill did the next best thing he could. He reached into the cabinet on the bulkhead of the control panel, and pulled out a bottle of Jim Beam Black and a glass. He dropped a shot of the Jim Beam into the glass, tipped it back slowly, and felt the relaxing sensation of the warm whiskey coating his throat. He would only drink as much as it took to clear his head.

Bill blinked twice, forcing his eyes to clear and focus on the water in front of him. It was imperative that he find the northern tributary for the Amazon, as he would never be able to challenge the mighty discharge at the mouth of the Amazon. His best chance was to cross around it, go north and continue upstream until the water became calm. He had two more hours to go, and then he would be relieved for six hours.

The Atlantic aspect of the Caribbean was cold at night, and Bill shivered in spite of himself. He thought back to the day he had left the Lost El Dorado and his friend John Waales. He knew he had to get back there. Also, he needed to try to find the prisoner Thomas Reichen and take his security personally.

Dark water was ahead of him and there were low clouds on the horizon, which was lit by a full moon. He studied the chart that was spread out on the control panel above the wheel, and also at the navigation/GPS combination, which was leading him toward the great continent of South America. Bill sighed in spite of himself. Yet another trek up the Amazon, but this one without pay. Fortunately, the last journey had paid well enough so that he could afford the fuel and ammo he would need.

He thought about the past year. His close personal friend, probably his best friend, John Waales, the archaeologist from U. C. Berkeley back in the States, had called him. He wanted to take another run at finding the famous Lost El Dorado. The first try wound up in disaster, almost costing them their lives. But the second try, last year, almost fared no better. While they had found some success, they had almost been killed again.

He shook his head. What a mess that was! They had John's friend Jack, a chiropractor, on-board. Surprisingly, he became a bad-ass when they needed help in battle; John's teenage daughter Kimmiko, also helped them at the end. The quest had been successful, but not without great personal cost, which made this situation a threat to John.

He then stayed behind to continue to explore the lost mines

and tunnels, that were much more complicated. The local host natives, eventually grew tired of John's presence and began to hate him after a while. The main instigator, Thomas Reichen, an ex-CIA spy and trained killer, who had tried to take the gold and kill them all, was now loose and would probably come back for revenge. Bill had taken him downriver as a prisoner and turned him over to the authorities for punishment. But he had escaped, and was probably plotting his revenge.

Bill had already purchased two more torpedoes and also the depth charges he had used in battle, with the rewards he had gotten from the last expedition - not to mention the .50 mm bullets for the twin machine guns, and the ordnance for the Oerlikon cannon. 20 mm ammo did not come cheap, especially in this part of the world. Now, he needed additional food and water. He also had to contact Manolo, his former mate on the last, and many other expeditions. The guys on board with him now were competent enough for a treasure hunt, but not for possibly going into battle.

He thought that the natives, and John's situation were stable now, and that they were all safe there. He had no idea how wrong he was, but he was soon to find out.

****

Chief Damien Omagua of the Chibcha Tribe laughed as he threw his baby daughter high up into the air and caught her just before she reached the ground. His daughter, Cornelia, squealed in delight at the game. Only two years old, she was enthralled with her daddy and her mommy. The three of them played on the beach, in the shadow of the gold temples and buildings of the

City of the Lost El Dorado.

Only a year before, they would never have dared come close to this beach, as there had been monster piranha fish, some as long as 15 feet, who were ferocious man-eaters. The piranha were gone now, most of them dead because of the battle for the village between the good and bad Chibchas tribes, the PT boat that fought them, and also an elongated hunt by the new Chibcha tribe, who wanted them gone.

The village was good now. The white men from the North, who had helped liberate their village, had been allowed to explore their village and their jungle. They had extracted several thousand pounds of gold for their efforts. In exchange, of course, they had helped the tribal natives obtain things they needed for the tribe. These white men were cooperative and pleasant, even keeping the location of the village a secret, for even they did not want the world to know exactly where the gold mines were.

The leader, John Waales, an important Professor from the University of California Berkeley, in the United States, was very nice and treated them with respect. Although he had been there a year and had brought in a couple of his closest colleagues, he still kept most of the project's secrets to himself. The plan was to work for one-to -three more years and then leave. They would only share so much with the world about their findings.

Chief Damien, who at 21, was quite young to lead such an important tribe of the Chibchas, set his daughter down on the warm sand. She began to run around him in circles. He and his wife, Patricia, smiled down at her. He frowned for a moment.

The problem was his sister, Princess Cornelia and her husband, Prince Mondo, who were newly reunited with Chief Damien and the tribe. The couple had been exiled by their father Chief Sanek Omagua when they were both fifteen, which was fifteen years earlier, and also by their wicked older brother, Prince Sajava, who wanted to do evil things with the fish and the surrounding tribes.

He, then a very young Prince Damien, at the age of five, had been spared harm by their mother, who had now passed away. The Prince had been obedient to his father and older brother, although he was afraid of them and their power. He was especially terrified of the giant piranha, who would eat their very flesh if they were given the chance.

Princess Cornelia and her husband Prince Mondo were happy to be living back among their fellow tribesmen, but they had grown weary of the outsiders, like Professor Waales - even though they would not be here now without him. They had had many meetings and discussions far into the night about how they would handle the outsiders. It was, after all, their land and their tribe.

Damien sat down in the warm sand and began tickling his daughter, one of her favorite games. She laughed and howled in protest. Then Chief Damien hugged her tight and forgot all about everything except her, his wife and the warm sand they were resting on.

****

Thomas Reichen had to proceed carefully. After he had left the jungle, he had made his way to Bogota, Colombia. He changed his appearance and had a new I.D. and passport made. He bought a plane ticket to the United States - based on false documentation

– and boarded the plane at 6 A.M for the eight-hour flight to San Francisco.

Sitting in the back seat of a private limousine, Reichen contemplated his life so far and the events, that had led him here. A CIA operative and clandestine assassin during the Vietnamese War, he had sanctioned many "bad guys." Once the trajectory of the war began to turn, however, and the opportunity for him to extract large quantities of cocaine and other drugs began to emerge, he had also sanctioned a lot of "good guys."

It became apparent when the fortunes of war began to run out, that the people who controlled him were beginning to look for new cash cows, before they were forced to leave Southeast Asia forever. There were hundreds of tons of raw cocaine coming out of the jungles of Viet Nam and also the mountains of the surrounding countries which needed to be controlled. Thomas Reichen had no scruples about killing and had his own agenda of limitless greed. The situation suited him perfectly and he used the profits from selling cocaine to position him as a major player in Columbia.

While he was actually too high of an operative to engage in local "drug deals," it actually excited him to no end to still be a "ground player." So, he would make deals, some which were clean, and some which required his own definition of justice to make sure he personally did not lose out. This meant that he got profits from drug runners who wanted to keep doing business with him, or dealt death to bad guys who wanted to rip him off. It was all in good fun, after all!

The plane had landed at San Francisco Airport, and a "Mr. Worthy" had met him at the gate. The man was professional and courteous, although Reichen doubted his sincerity after he was pushed, rather roughly into the stretch limo.

Mr. Worthy did not accompany Reichen, but assured him there was plenty of ice and liquor available in the limo, as well as an excellent Reuben sandwich under the warming plate, with corned beef and Swiss cheese from Sonoma County in California, sauerkraut from Germany, and dressing flown in from Russia. Plus, there was Dijon mustard on the side. Reichen smiled and poured himself a Johnny Walker Blue Label Scotch, worth $120.00 per bottle, and soda on the rocks. He ate and drank with gusto as the limousine rolled over the San Francisco Bay Bridge and into the East Bay Area.

Reichen had heard about a person, who might help him with his situation in Columbia. He wanted to get back to the El Dorado Village, take the gold and kill both Professor Waales and Captain Bill Treese. Reichen had been told the man lived in the wealthy suburb of Blackhawk, in Danville, approximately 20 miles from Berkeley. The name given to him was only Charley, which caused a mixture of amusement and worry, because "Charley" was the term they used in the Vietnam War for the North Vietnamese soldiers. The US Military would use the "Phonetic Alphabet", so that the Viet Cong (Vietnamese Communists or VC), were referred to as "Victor Charley", or "Charley" for short. He wasn't sure if this meeting was going to be with a former military enemy, or someone else.

Nor was his worry mitigated as they were stopped at the gated community by a guard who viewed them with some suspicion when the driver named the person they were coming to see. After more questioning, they were finally allowed through the East Gate and sent on their way.

Now, as they progressed by the manicured lawns of the enormous and ornate houses, past the two world-renowned golf courses and up into the highest reaches of Blackhawk, they finally stopped at a home more modest than he had imagined, but still grand in its own way.

The limousine was parked on the street below the house and Reichen walked up the curved, brick-lined walkway to an elegant glass-and-iron front door. As he rang the doorbell, he heard the pleasant chimes of Westminster.

After a few moments a small, mousy-looking man answered the door. Sallow- faced, he was wearing a black suit, white shirt and black tie.

"May I help you, sir?" he asked in a slight British accent.

Reichen, for no apparent reason, suddenly became very nervous. His hands started to shake. Since the man had not offered to shake his hand, Reichen kept both hands pressed tightly against his pants.

"Ah, yes. Thank you," Reichen stammered. "I am Thomas Reichen. I, uh, called earlier to meet with Mr. Charley."

"Yes sir. I am Jones. Please follow me to the Great Room." With that, Jones turned curtly and led Reichen through the simple entryway and into an ornate living room. Rich tapestries and oil paintings covered the walls; many depicted ancient scenes of hunting and battles of war. The floor was a rich mixture of marble and granite tiles, covered in places by thick Arabian rugs. A huge stone fireplace covered one entire wall and was two stories high. There was a fire burning, that smelled like oak logs. The furniture alone could pay for several journeys up the Amazon! Something told Thomas that this Great Room was only just the beginning.

"May I get you something sir? Coffee, tea, a cola, or, perhaps, an adult beverage?" Jones inquired of Reichen.

Reichen was still shaking slightly, which was completely out of character for him. He didn't know what to expect next. "Ah, no. Thank you."

Jones, the gentleman's gentleman - a term sometimes used in place of the term butler, nodded. "Please have a seat, sir," he said, motioning Thomas toward a large, elegant wood and green leather sofa near the fireplace. The request, however, came off as more of an order than an offer to be friendly.

Reichen sat down stiffly.

"The master will be with you shortly, sir."

Suddenly a voice behind Thomas said, "Well, here you are!"

Thomas jumped up, startled, and turned around.

Charlie was in her sixties, but could easily pass for forty. She was about 5'10", with blonde hair, and a body that showed she worked out religiously. Her face was flawless, her eye's half-closed. She wore an emerald-green gown, cut low in the front, highlighting her ample breasts and flowed down almost to the floor. Thomas saw she was wearing elegant gold, high-heeled pumps, as she walked toward him. She had a matching gold-and-diamond medallion on a heavy gold chain around her neck. In her hair was also a matching gold tiara.

"My apologies for having startled you," she chuckled. "Please sit down and let us talk."

She smiled as she walked over to a large earth globe, which was obviously hiding a bar. Opening the top and reaching inside, she pulled out a crystal decanter filled with an amber-colored liquid.

"You must try my brandy. It is 50 years old, and very special." She
smiled. Charlie selected two large Waterford crystal snifters and
poured each glass one-quarter full. She handed one to Thomas.
Looking directly into his eyes, she said, "To your quest," as she
raised her glass and drank deeply.

In spite of his advanced combat training, intelligence instincts,
and having been commander of an elite espionage unit, Reichen
found himself overwhelmed by everything happening all at once.
He gratefully drank the warm alcohol, which tasted smooth, but
burned his throat going down. He coughed, embarrassed and sat
back down.

Charlie smiled at him. "It is good, yes? My family has been
making this brandy for over two hundred years, here in America,
and before that, in Russia and South America." She turned and
stared into the fire. "You will get used to it," her voice trailed off.

She sat down next to Reichen on the couch. "So, you have
come to ask us for some minor assistance in your, how shall we say
it....quest?"

"Yes," he answered, "I saw the treasure. It was thwarted from
me and I need to get it back. The buildings alone are worth a
100,000,000. I need $500,000 to reclaim it, and another $500,000
to get it taken apart and transported out of there. If I have to get
a Huey, it might cost another 2 or 3 million with a local pilot, but
that's for later on. There was a drop spot in the jungle the last time
I was there, but it may be grown over now. I have landmarks to get
us there, but it is always tricky in the jungle."

"Are you still hurting because a mere professor of archaeology
from Berkeley slayed you?" she asked, sinking back into the couch
with a bemused look on her face.

He looked at her sharply. "How did you know that..?" his voice trailing off.

"Oh, I hear things." she smiled at him teasingly.

Reichen looked down heavily. He put the snifter on a side table next to him, then wiped his brow with his hands for several seconds. "Yes," he said with a sigh, "That's what is tearing me apart. I had the fortune, I had the Indians, and I had the people in place to take it all. Then it slipped through my grasp and the whole thing fell apart. The next thing I knew, I was a prisoner and was heading back to civilization in chains."

"I am willing to finance your adventure. I have my terms, which will be explained to you. But don't worry, they are very generous. However, you must show me your data you have so far. After all, we both know what happened the last time." She paused, "I want you to be safe, Mr. Reichen," she said, smiling softly.

Two hours later, as Thomas Reichen slid into the limousine to catch his plane for the ride back to South America, he had a plan – best of all, he also had the support he needed.

Inside the house, Charlie, sat down again on the rich leather sofa, Thomas had been sitting on earlier. She sipped the last of her brandy from her snifter.

"You can come out now," she said to someone in the study to her right.

The door opened and a tall, heavily built man came out and stood before her. He was the Financier.

"Well, Andres, what did you think?" she asked him.

He smiled at her. Almost 70 years old, his jowls jiggled slightly when he talked. "First, where's that brandy?" he asked, almost rudely. At six feet tall and weighing over 280 pounds, Andres was sweating in the warm living room. He sat down heavily in an adjoining armchair.

Charlie motioned with her chin to the large mobile globe bar. It showed an ancient map of the world on it, from the Christopher Columbus era. Andres hesitated for a moment, as though he expected her to get the drink for him. She looked away at the view of Mt. Diablo from her perfectly situated sofa. With a grunt, he finally got up and crossed the room to the bar. Pouring himself an almost-full glass, he dropped two large ice cubes into the oversize brandy snifter. Charlie looked at him, squinted her eyes, and shook her head in disapproval.

"Ice, with 50-year-old brandy? You've got to be kidding!"

"Sorry, it's hot in here. I even put ice in my red wine!"

Charlie turned away in disgust and gazed out the window again. "Why don't you just drink a damn beer?" she asked as she rolled her eyes. "Well, what do you think of him?" she repeated.

"I think he can do the job, with the right support coming from us. I don't like the terms, however. A 50/50 split of the profits, but we have to put up the front money? I know I have my resources that can help us, but what do you have?"

Almost on cue, a young, native girl appeared out of the shadows..

Charlie stood up, went to her and embraced her. "My daughter, Zenadia" she said to Andres the Financier. "My resource."

Zenadia was about 5' tall, slender at the hips, with wide shoulders. She wore a tight-fitting, animal print top, and she appeared to be rather buxom. She wore some kind of a native skirt, which cascaded down to her knees. Her feet and legs were bare. What appeared to be a curved bone or tooth, secured by a black leather band, a necklace was above her chest. A bone clip held her bangs back, while the rest of her hair cascaded wildly down her back, to her buttocks. Her skin was a dark chestnut-brown. It appeared as though the blood coursing through her arteries pulsed right through her face. Her nostrils flared, as she looked at the Financier. The contrast between her and her mother Charlie could not have been more pronounced.

For his part, Andres was taken aback. A man of great wealth and property, few people could make him speechless, or embarrass him in any way. But this girl/woman, or, as he thought inwardly of her, wild animal, did. He also felt a definite pressure in his groin when he looked at her. God only knew how old she was.

As if she could read his thoughts, Zenadia smiled coyly at Andres. "My mother says you are our friend and partner in this adventure."

He tilted his head toward her. It was as if she didn't speak, but yet was putting words into his head. Zenadia had a slight Spanish accent, mixed with some sort of South American Indian. He suddenly felt as if she had put him into a trance, then shook his head and quickly snapped out of it.

"Yes, yes. I want this to happen as badly as you do, but it is an investment. Investments must be carefully planned, they must be carefully controlled, and they must be carefully watched over."

Zenadia stepped slowly away from her mother. She looked at the Financier and smiled, saying, "Don't worry about it." With that, she spun away and disappeared, leaving Andres speechless.

Charlie smiled and looked up at the Financier. She had seen that reaction to her "daughter" before from other men. "Better start making some phone calls," she said clearly, as she walked over to the large picture window.

****

Bill Treese had finally found the entry to the Amazon he was looking for. The word he had received was that he had to pick up a doctor in a village near Bogota, and get him to the El Dorado as fast as he could. There was a very sick child that needed his attention and a certain medication immediately. The child was getting worse by the day, and nobody knew know how long he had to live.

Thomas Reichen would just have to wait.

Treese had stopped at an outpost in Brazil and released Carlos and Miguel. Julian had stayed with him, since he was a good gunner and could also drive the boat. In spite of his youth, he knew the river well and was a good man, who could be counted on in an emergency.

Bill Treese had also picked up his young friend Manolo, who had sailed with him many times before. Manolo had been with them on the last voyage to the Village of the Lost El Dorado.

Manolo and Julian had met each other a few years before and worked together, so there was no drama between them. The question of which one was First Mate never came up, nor was it important on Bill's boat.

It was now morning. The clouds on the river were relatively light and they were making good headway against the tide. Manolo appeared on deck.

"Breakfast is ready, sir!" He snapped a salute.

"Cut that out, Manolo. No need for that, ya! Did Julian eat

yet?"

"No, *Capitán* Bill. He said for you to eat first, then we will both eat. He will be here to drive the boat in a minute."

"Okay, okay," Bill smiled and turned back to the river. A minute later, Julian bounded up the ladder.

"Good morning *Capitán* Bill," he said with a huge smile. "Reporting as ordered!"

Bill smiled. "I didn't order you, but thanks for the relief," he said as he started down the ladder to the small galley below. Suddenly he turned and said to Julian, "How the heck do you keep your hair so spiky in all this heat?" Then he grinned to show he was just kidding.

"Spiky, creamy stuff from the U.S.! Works even in this heat!"

Bill laughed, shook his head and went below.

****

Princess Cornelia, the sister to Chief Damien and wife of Prince Mondo, stared out at the Amazon River. Not even the luster of the gold buildings that were built centuries ago, and searched for, for over a thousand years, could lift her spirits. It is true, she thought, that the Americans had helped reunite the two estranged tribes, however, her heart was still heavy.

The Americans needed to leave now, although they had only been here one year, and had been promised at least three years of exploration. There had been muttering among the tribal leaders, and open complaints from the natives, that they wanted to be left alone to raise their families, grow their crops and hunt fish. There was even talk, never in front of her or her brother and husband, of overthrowing them, the leaders, and killing or kicking out the Americans.

Her husband was away leading a fishing expedition for a couple of weeks, so Princess Cornelia decided to go and see her brother, Chief Damien.

As she walked over the now-familiar tracks to his hut, she could hear him playing with his daughter Cornelia, who was named after her. Princess Cornelia smiled at the memory of when she and her brother met again last year for the first time in years. Her father, Chief Omagua, had cursed her and her husband and banished them from the village a long time ago. When the Princess and her husband had attacked with the Americans, she found her brother and met his wife and their new baby girl.

Their fifteen-year exile had been hard, but there was a price on Princess Cornelia's and her husband's heads. They were married a year later, when they were both just sixteen. She had sent secret word to her mother, whom she loved and missed desperately, that she was now married, and had had her babies early. In fact, she had six children before Little Prince Damien had been born. Her mother had passed away five years after her exile and the news had devastated Princess Cornelia. As far as her father and oldest brother went, she spat on the ground every night before bed and prayed for their imminent deaths.

She smiled as she knocked on the door of her brother's home. She could hear peals of laughter coming from her little niece, inside the hut.

"You may enter," Chief Damien called out.

She opened the door and stepped in. It took her a few seconds to adjust to the dim light inside, lit by torches. She could see that her brother had been pretending to tickle baby Cornelia's feet as she shrieked with delight. One real tickle was all it took, then 10 minutes of pretend tickling, all of which she anticipated with gleeful happiness.

"Sister!" Chief Damien cried out when he saw her. "Why aren't you preparing for your husband's return, with his usual boatload of fish?"

"And why aren't you, my brother the Chief, holding court with your worthy subjects instead of tickling your daughter without mercy?"

They both laughed. But as he looked at her, his smile faded.

"Something is troubling you, is it not, my sister?"

She looked down. "Yes, my brother."

"Well, what then?"

Princess Cornelia got down on her knees, next to her brother, and looked into his eyes. "It's the Americans," she said softly. "The tribe wants them out. They feel we can handle any outside aggressions ourselves and we should be left alone." She looked away, knowing how her brother felt.

"Cornelia, they helped us in ways we can never repay. We would be dead now if it was up to our father and brother. I too look forward to when we can be left alone. But the Americans have only been here one year, out of the three that we promised."

"Three years we agreed to. Not promised!" she said as she watched him. "I know I am being unreasonable, my brother, but many in the tribe are unhappy. There has even been loose talk about some of our tribesmen overthrowing us and then killing the Americans to keep them silent."

Damien was quiet. He looked away from her as though he

were searching back in time to a period of fear, murder and torture by their father, brother and the evil giant piranha.

He looked fondly at his sister, whom he had missed dearly and did not have a chance to grow up with. Also, he missed their dead mother, who died of a broken heart at the loss of her daughter and family after they had been sent away by her cruel husband the King.

He held her shoulders as she looked into his eyes.

"Don't worry. I will talk to the tribe, your husband, the Council and the Americans. Perhaps a compromise can be reached."

Princess Cornelia smiled and hugged her brother tightly. "Always the man of reason," she said gratefully.

She got up and started to leave.

"You don't want to play with us?" Chief Damien asked as he resumed tickling Baby Cornelia's toes.

She smiled. "I would stay, but your nephew, my son Damien, has not been well these past couple of days, and I need to get back to him.

"Thank you," she said quietly as she left, leaving Chief Damien to play with his daughter, but now with a much heavier heart than a few minutes ago.

****

Kimmiko Waales, the 20-year-old daughter of John Waales, was fast asleep in her rented one-bedroom apartment in Berkeley. It was after midnight; she had been asleep for only 45 minutes when her cell phone began ringing. Because she had been studying all day for her midterms at U.C. Berkeley, she had dropped off into a deep sleep.

She reached for her cell phone, the need for sleep raging against her tired mind. As she held the phone in her hand, she lay down, closed her eyes tightly, so she could clear them. She opened her eyes and looked at the caller. What she saw made her shoot straight up in the dark; she quickly pressed the Accept Button on her cell phone and turned on the lamp beside her bed.

"Manolo!" she said excitedly. "Why are you calling me in the middle of the night from South America? Did you want to kiss and make up?" she giggled. She still had very strong feelings for him. If there was anyone she loved other than her father, her Uncle Bill Treese and her Uncle Jack Paris, it was probably Manolo. Even though they were both young, they had been through a lifetime together on that damn river, the Amazon, last year.

"Kimmi, Kimmi!" Manolo stammered. "There's been an accident with your father!"

Kimmiko Waales' blood ran cold. She almost dropped the phone. Her mother had passed away years ago, and her father had raised her as a single parent. An active archaeologist, he had to leave her alone many times while he went into the fields to do research.

"What happened?" she asked in a whisper.

"He was exploring the mine under the Lost El Dorado and there was a cave-in! He was by himself. It was at night. When he didn't show up, the native guards went out to look for him. The ground was still shaking and the entrance to the tunnel was blocked!"

In spite of herself, Kimmiko started sobbing. "I never should have left him and come back to school. I should have stayed!

Damnit!" She slammed her fist into the bed.

Controlling her emotions, she asked, "Where's Uncle Bill?"

"I am contacting him now. It is crazy, Kimmi. There is so much to tell you! Do you remember Princess Cornelia? And her husband Mondo? They have a baby named Prince Damien, named after her brother, the real now - Chief Damien, who is the leader of the Chibcha Tribe."

"Of course, I do. Why? Are they the ones who caused the cave-in?" Kimmi suddenly saw red as her mouth twisted into a grimace of anger and hate. "They wanted him out! He wrote me!"

"No, no. I don't think so. They contacted me as soon as they could, to tell me to get you, to help your dad. Their child, Prince Damien, has gotten very sick and no one seems to be able to help him. Every day, he is getting sicker. He may die if they can't help him. They have sent word to your Uncle Bill, my skipper, to pick up a doctor who is an expert in exotic diseases and bring medicine to help him. The PT boat can get there in three days, at full speed. You have to fly into Bogota tonight and get here by morning! You should call your Uncle Jack and bring him. You can be picked up by *Capitán* Bill the next morning. We can rendezvous on the river. I can meet you there." I will send you the details. Do you have your passport?"

"Yes. Manolo, I have to go. I'll call Uncle Jack and book the flights. Text me where we can meet you. Thank you." She hesitated a moment. "Monolo…" her voice drifted off. "I still…" but she couldn't finish her sentence, as she was suddenly overcome by a rush of emotions.

For the first time, Manolo sounded energized, "Me too!" he

said, with happiness in his voice. "See you soon!" and then he was gone.

****

It was even later when Dr. Jack Paris' cell phone rang next to his bed. He was a light sleeper, and he picked it up immediately.

"Kimmi!" he said. "What's going on?" She quickly related the story to him. Jack sighed. It was never easy in these Third World countries. "I will get tickets for us immediately. I'll call you when I have our flight arranged. We may have to do some of the connections on the drive over to the airport, but it should be okay." She thanked him, gratefully.

He touched his sleeping wife Lisa on her bare shoulder. She rolled over and looked at him sleepily.

"I have to fly to Bogota in the morning. John's been involved in a cave-in, and it doesn't look good. I'm picking up Kimmiko and we need to be on the first flight into Bogota. Bill is going to pick us up on the boat and take us to the El Dorado."

Lisa fell back onto her pillow, fully awake. "Jeez, Jack, not back into that hell-hole again?!"

"No. There are no bad guys. Just an effort to get John out. I'll be back in a week. Please don't worry. I love you!"

He jumped out of bed to search for the earliest plane to Bogota, Colombia.

Lisa sighed. "Love you too," she whispered. How little they both knew that this trip would be the worst of all.

CHAPTER TWO

THE AMAZON

THE PAST, ALMOST 24 HOURS, had been tough for Jack Paris and Kimmiko Waales. They had been making plans and booking flights on their phones while driving to San Francisco International Airport. Finally, they boarded a flight to Bogota, Colombia that left at 6 A.M. and arrived in Bogota 9 hours later. There they had to wait two hours to board a flight to Leticia, also known as *Tres Fronteras*, because of the three countries of Brazil, Colombia and Peru all came together there. That lasted another 2 1/4 hours. Then, hot, tired, hungry and thirsty, they took a taxi to the dock, where Bill was supposed to meet them with the PT boat.

It was just before 11 P.M. The boat wasn't at the dock yet. A late-night bar/food room was still open. Jack and Kimmi had traveled light and walked into the patio of the bar carrying their bags. A handful of rough-looking men and no women were inside. Probably, the men were dock workers who were getting off late.

Feeling like a couple of cherries on top of a cream pie, Jack and Kimmi walked past the staring men to a table near the back of the room and sat down nervously. After about five minutes, the bartender approached them. He was short, heavy and totally bald. "What can I get for you?" he asked in Spanish.

Jack replied, in Spanish, "Is there food? We are meeting a friend here on the docks tonight."

"*Si,*" came the reply. "*Torta ahogadas.*"

"Can we have two, please? Along with two beers. I only have American currency. Will that be okay?"

"*Si.*"

"What did you order?" asked Kimmi?"

"Pork sandwiches. Probably fried, like carnitas. Hopefully, they'll be good."

One minute later, they heard the distinctive sound of a microwave starting; soon they were served two pulled pork carnitas sandwiches, wrapped in white butcher paper, slathered in salsa rosada, or pink sauce, with onions and chilies, along with two *BBC Septimazo IPA's*, an excellent local beer from the Bogota Beer Company. The sandwiches were actually rather good. There was local mustard and more red-hot sauce, which livened things up. Since they were hungry, they ate, but did not speak. When they finished, they just sat there waiting.

Jack did not know what they were going to do if Bill did not show up soon. After a while, most of the men had left. Two men seated across the barroom had been staring on and off at Jack and Kimmi. They looked like locals, meaning they looked and dressed rough.

Jack eventually got up and asked the bartender, who was drying beer glasses at the counter, what time he closed.

"In about one hour," came the reply.

"Okay, thanks. Is there a bathroom?

"Down the hall to the back."

Jack went over to get Kimmi. He didn't want to leave her alone. "Let's go back to the bathroom together. We can wait in the hall for each other."

Afterwards, back at the table again, they nursed their beers slowly. The bartender came up and surprisingly sat down at their table.

"I am Luis," he said in English. I am the owner. You two are a long way from home. Who are you waiting for? This can be a dangerous place."

Then the bell on the front door jingled and the two remaining men left. One of the men turned around, looking at Jack and Kimmi, tipped his brimmed straw hat, smiled and winked. He then turned and followed his companion out into the warm and humid night.

"What was all of that about?" asked Jack.

"They are local pilots. They fly crop dusters, jungle retardants. Maybe cocaine, but that's the rumor. I don't ask. They come in, eat, pay their bill and go."

"Speaking of which, how much for the food?"

"$15.00 US."

Jack gave him a twenty-dollar bill. "Keep the change. Is there a safe place we can stay until our boat arrives?"

"Boat? At this time at night?" he said incredulously. "It's dangerous on the Amazon, especially at night. What boat?"

"Bill Treese."

"The PT boat?"

"Yes." I can't raise him because my cell phone won't work down here."

Luis smiled. "Hang on a minute." He went into the kitchen and was gone almost ten minutes. Jack and Kimmi were getting nervous.

Luis returned to their table. "He'll be here in a half hour."

"Wait, how did you…?" Jack's voice trailed off.

"I radioed him. He's a friend. You can wait here until he arrives. He'll probably have a couple of beers and sleep in the back or on board his boat until morning.

Want another beer?"

"No thanks," Jack said.

Kimmi spoke up for the first time. "Could we have some water, please?"

Luis smiled and bowed his head at her, respectful of the pretty young lady, whom he hoped was a daughter of this American, and not something else.

What Jack and Kimmi did not see, was that the two men who had just left the bar, were now on the side of the building, standing in the shadows, watching them through the windows. They had been waiting for these two *gringos* to come into town. They had almost given up, so they went into the bar for drinks and some food. Just when they were about to leave, the door opened and there were the *gringos*.

"The boat is coming in, *amigo*. The Americans have paid us well, but there is much more money to come if we sink this boat and kill these *gringos*!"

"*Si*. Target practice begins at dawn!" They fell back into the shadows and into the darkness.

****

Princess Cornelia hurried back to her house, one of the more ornate ones made of gold near the river. Her heart was troubled, not just by the conversation she had just had with her brother, Chief Damien, about the Americans here, but also because she was worried about her young son, also named Prince Damien after her brother.

They had not seen each other since they were young, because of their father, Chief Omagua and her brother, Prince Sajava. Her father had put a price of death on her head and also that of her husband, Mondo, and they had escaped the village of the El Dorado with their lives.

As she went through the door, she called for her son's nurse to come out.

"How is my son?" she asked.

The elderly woman, named Sabria said, "Not much has changed. He is still sleeping. His color is still good, but he sleeps all day and all night. His breathing may be getting less strong, but nothing terrible. He just won't wake up."

Cornelia's brow wrinkled. She walked into her son's room, and looked down at him in his small bed. He was only a little over two years old. He looked peaceful. But that is what unnerved her. He should be playing and running furiously, like he had been doing a week ago. There were no spider bites, no falls, no fevers, nothing to indicate what had happened to him. He had gone to bed two days ago, and had not awakened since.

Becoming emotional, she started to cry in spite of herself. A mother's intuition, she clutched her fists to her breast. Trying to make the anxiety pass, she fell to her knees, dropped her head and began to pray. Christianity was not lost on her! She prayed to God and to Jesus. Sobbing, she wished that Mondo, her husband, would get home. Something was terribly wrong with their son and she didn't know what it was.

There was the internet. And there were cell phones. But there was no way to get in touch with her husband, to tell him to get home because of the dangers in this third-world jungle.

****

Kimmi and Jack had fallen asleep with their heads resting on the table in the bar. The owner, Luis, had, mercifully, found some paperwork to do in the back, so he let them sleep until Bill Treese would arrive and fetch them onto his PT boat. They were safe here in the bar, but not out by the docks.

The night was still and warm. Not too hot, but humid. Out of the darkness, Luis heard the rumblings of the PT boat as it moved into the dock outside. He smiled and looked at his watch. It was 2:15 AM. And it would take about 10 minutes for Bill to come inside, so he went back to his books.

Exactly at 2:25 A.M., the outside screen door opened suddenly with a crash! Bill Treese leapt inside. "Where's my favorite niece, and my favorite chiropractor?!" he bellowed.

Startled, Jack and Kimmi jumped to their feet as though hit by lightning. Then both of them fell back, laughing, as Bill rushed over and hugged them in his big muscular arms.

"Ok, Ok, Ok!" Bill said. "Sorry about that! No time for hugs and kisses. We have to leave immediately." He looked, concerned at Kimmi. "Your dad needs us right now. Plus, there is a new problem. I'll fill you in when we get on the boat. So, grab your gear and let's go!"

Luis hurried out of the back, with a classic bartender's towel draped over his shoulder, even though he had been doing paperwork.

Bill gave him a big smile. "*Amigo*, thanks for looking out for my family!" he said.

Luis smiled. "Bad eyes in here tonight, if you know what I mean." He looked Bill directly in the eye. "Your friends have been seen and identified. I suggest you take a different route, if you know what I mean." They both knew there was a tributary on the Amazon that would lengthen their trip by a day, but would be much safer for them.

Bill smiled and looked down. "No-can-do *Padre*. Fastest route possible. Into harm's way once again!" He looked down and shook his head. The danger never ended.

"*Si. Via con dios, amigo.*" Go with God, friend. "You want a beer?"

Bill smiled. "I would love one, but I need to drive." They both laughed, knowing he meant the boat.

Luis heaved up a huge carafe of coffee and set it on the bar. "It's good. Real Colombian coffee. Not that Navy shit you like to pour!"

"Ha, ha. Got it! But my coffee is hot, good, and it keeps me awake. For hours," Bill added. "But just to be polite..." he reached for the coffee gratefully. He reached into his pocket to get some money.

"Luis held up his hand. "You can pay me later, Bill Treese," he said, as he disappeared back into his office.

****

Bill's PT boat cruised at medium-to-full speed the rest of the night. He had allowed Jack and Kimmi to go below to get some much-needed sack time before dawn. Manolo, after a happy and tearful reunion with Kimmi, also went to sleep. The plan was for Julian Jonas, Bill's current First Mate, to drive the boat for a few hours, but Bill was too amped-up to rest. He couldn't sleep if he tried. Luis' coffee was good. Damn good. It helped keep him awake. It was almost dawn, and they had put in over thirty miles from Leticia down the Amazon heading east.

Bill saw that the clouds of the night were beginning to clear. The sun started to shine over the river, rising in the East. That's when Bill saw them approach.

Two Japanese WWII fighter planes, the Mitsubishi A6M, also known as the Japanese Zero, had lifted off from the airport at Leticia. Banking sharply, they headed into the sunrise. Flying low along the Amazon, they saw their target in just a few minutes. As they pulled up sharply on their yokes, the two Colombian pilots from the night before, banked upwards and flew directly into the sunrise. Always good gunfighters, they knew they had to attack the PT boat with the sun at their backs. They flew in uniform fashion up to 10,000 feet, and then ten miles forward, to the PT boat's position.

Curling back into attack position, they were now on a direct path to the PT boat. As they lowered their left wings, they went into a free-fall dive, their engines screaming and hit the hard deck 100 feet above the Amazon, approaching the PT boat at over 300 miles per hour!

Bill heard the planes when they rose into the air. In spite of the roar of the PT boat's engines, he had been trained in combat. Also, Bill knew this part of the river well and there was no way that what he heard was natural.

He immediately threw the "General Quarters "lever. As the box started screaming out the General Quarters bells, Bill shouted over the boat's intercom, "General Quarters! General Quarters! This is no Drill!! This is no Drill!!"

From below deck, out came Jack, Manolo, Julian and Kimmiko. "What the hell is happening?" Jack screamed.

Bill had no time for formalities. "Jack, you are on the starboard gun on the right. Manolo, on the left gun. Julian, get on the Oerlikon cannon. Kimmi get down next to me; I may need you. Everybody, get on life jackets and helmets. Now!!!

They all jumped into action. "Look ahead and into the clouds," Bill said. "We're about to be attacked!"

Suddenly, they heard the two planes making their attack run on the boat. The Mitsubishi engines screamed. As they descended, the fighter planes opened up machine gun fire on the PT boat.

Tracer bullets landed in front of the boat and proceeded to strafe up and to the side. Several hit the foredeck of the PT boat and then continued down the middle to the bridge. Kimmi screamed and tucked herself into the bridge area. Bill crouched down at the helm. He had reinforced the bridge and the two gun turrets with heavy bulletproof steel and Kevlar mesh. Only Julian, on the cannon in the stern of the boat was exposed. He never knew what happened as rounds from the two 7.7mm machine guns hit him in the chest and he flew off the boat, mortally wounded.

Bill jumped up and juked the boat to the side, lest they be blown out of the water.

As the planes passed overheard, Jack and Manolo, were staring at the planes in stunned silence. "Wake the fuck up!" Bill screamed at them. "Fire on those sons of bitches! They just killed Julian!"

Immediately, Manolo and Jack raised their .50 mm twin machine guns and began to fire at the escaping planes. Once the planes were out of sight, the two men lowered their weapons.

Then the two planes flew back into the sun at 3,000 feet, until they were, once again, ahead of the PT boat.

Bill screamed at them, "You fuckin' Cherries! They're coming back!" Just then, they heard the screaming engines of the two planes flying directly toward them, guns blazing.

Both Jack and Manolo raised their guns and took aim. "Manolo," Jack screamed above the roar of the engines, as Bill had pushed the throttle forward and the boat was now doing 50 knots, "Shoot at anything. Don't pick one. Just shoot!!"

The boat powered forward, even with the imminent possibility of the hull being ripped to pieces by damage from logs and trees that were floating in the Amazon.

They all saw the planes coming down, both barrels blazing at the PT boat. Bill juked the boat, and then sped up so the bullets would fly harmlessly over them. As the planes passed overhead, Jack and Manolo fired at the planes and spun around. The twin .50 caliber machine guns on the PT boat, fired over two thousand rounds-per- minute. As the tracer fire reached up into the sky, following the plane on the right, it was apparent that the pilot had taken fire. Suddenly smoke was coming from the engine of the Zero. It climbed up, up and up, heeled over and dove out of sight over the canopy of the jungle. Then they heard a crash, and an explosion.

The other plane banked and began to come back, straight toward the PT boat! Bill juked it and made a hard turn to his port side, trying to get away. Jack and Manolo ducked down in their turrets. After the turn, they both spun their guns around to face the back of the boat, as the Zero approached, firing his guns.

They both opened up and again had to duck as the plane passed overhead, but without hitting the boat.

Once again, Bill spun the boat around, now traveling the opposite way down the river. As the plane flew upward, preparing to turn around and resume its attack, everyone was surprised when Kimmi, who had moved carefully backwards to the Oerlikon cannon, whipped the strap across her shoulders and opened up fire directly on the climbing plane. "POM! POM! POM!" the cannon sounded. Jack and Manolo started firing as well. No more than 10 seconds later, the telltale smoke from the engine of the escaping plane showed it was mortally wounded. They all continued to fire into the hull of the plane, sealing its fate. Suddenly the plane turned and began to charge straight at the PT boat!

"It's a kamikaze! "screamed Bill. They stood there helplessly as the plane dove, approaching the boat! Suddenly, it passed over the PT by 20 feet, as everyone on the deck flattened out. The plane crashed 200 yards in front of the boat, and exploded with a mighty thunder. Bill turned the boat sharply and pushed it forward as the plane rocked the boat up and down while the crew hung on.

After a short while it was all over.

****

Professor John Waales had been asleep for several hours. The rock that hit his head was not big enough to be fatal, or to cause any serious damage, but it was enough to knock him out. He opened his eyes, then reflexively closed them again, as if to hide from anyone or anything that might want to hurt him.

After a few seconds, Waales opened his eyes and began to look around. It was totally dark, but he immediately remembered he had been in a cave-in, and reached around to his emergency miners' flashlight, which hung at his side. He was lying on his stomach and there was a terrible weight on his legs. He found the miners' flashlight and moved it up his body to his side. He found the button, that turned on the switch and it snapped on.

The light flared up and shone outward. As he looked around, he realized the hopelessness of his situation. He was now wedged between the wall that he had seen before the cave-in and a new one, which had just appeared in front of him. He was able to roll over onto his back. As he scanned the new sheer rock wall, which looked to be over two stories high, his breath suddenly caught.

He found himself staring at what appeared to be a gold vein-as wide as a car and at least ten feet high-stretching back inside the wall God only knew how far.

John exhaled slowly. The sheer mass of the gold in front of him could be worth several hundred million dollars! Or, depending on how far back the gold went into the rock, the vein could be worth several billion dollars. "Or even more," he thought incredulous.

He took a deep breath. First things first; he had to survive and reached down to move whatever was covering up his legs. There were several rocks, that could be easily removed, one at a time. Once his legs were free, he was able to scoot forward under the archway into the small tunnel that had been created by the cave-in. His head hurt and he was disoriented by the shadows of darkness and light.

He took another deep breath, then reached down for his canteen of water. He attempted to stand up, but made it only to his knees, then took a long drink of the cool water, which helped clear his head. After a few minutes he was actually able to stand up. Using his emergency miners' flashlight, he was able to locate his heavy-duty flashlight, which had over one million candlepower. As he regained his feet, he swung his flashlight up, down, left and right.

In spite of the wall of gold, it looked like he was sealed in completely. Looking back, beyond the partially collapsed wall, he could see several tons of rock, blocking his way back up the shaft. He looked up at the ceiling of the cave, but could not see a way out.

He decided to go and inspect the gold wall. It was soft, compared to the rock around it, which indicated it could be pure 24 karat gold, instead of gold ore, which was almost unheard-of. This excited him even though it appeared he could be trapped there with his treasure forever. He knew the river was close by, but he was a little disoriented as to where. So, he sat down on a rock and began to think.

For whatever reason, he was still breathing - but who knew how long that would last? In fact, it seemed more air was coming in since the cave in. There was air before, but it was deep and musty, appropriate for a deep cave that had no way out. He raised his head and sniffed the air. No doubt about it, the air was fresher than before and slightly cooler too, which was something unusual for this jungle and its steamy heat. He hoped that wasn't a fissure leading to the Amazon River or its tributary running parallel to the cave. If so, the air could weaken the walls and cause a second cave-in, that one would fill the shaft with tons of water from the river.

He shook his head. Better to stay positive, he thought to himself.

Suddenly, he heard a clanking sound deep past the walls, as if coming from inside. He could not make out what it was, but it had to be man-made. He listened intently, but then it stopped, as if it knew he was listening. For the first time he shivered, in spite of the heat, at the thought of what might be out there. He felt a deep bone chill, and almost let out a scream of terror, even though there was nothing apparently there.

He quickly got ahold of himself, and forced his professional mind to discipline itself and look for a way out, even if it meant going past the Clanking Two-Headed Monster. He smiled for a second, but then the smile vanished as the faint clanking began again. He froze and turned off his flashlights, as if the darkness could help him hear better. Then there was no sound.

Wearily, he sat down again and leaned against a rock. In spite of his fear, the heat and his dire predicament, he dozed off and slept again.

CHAPTER THREE

CHARLIE

THE WIND OFF MT. DIABLO in the San Francisco East Bay had been howling all night. The rain started just after midnight, and by 12:30 A.M., a full-fledged storm had begun, with sheets of rain coming down without mercy.

In her home in Blackhawk, Charlie had not slept in two days, since Thomas Reichen left to return to the jungle with support from her and her Financier. She stood by the window, staring out into the dark night, knowing there were things she had to do. Slowly, she sipped her family's brandy.

Her mind drifted back to Viet Nam. Charlie was there towards the end of the war, as a CIA agent in charge of extracting information, soldiers, North Viet Cong prisoners and anyone or anything else that would help the U.S. and the South Vietnamese.

She was good at her job. She had trained at Camp Peary in Virginia, at the covert CIA training facility known as "The Farm." It was officially referred to as the Armed Forces Experimental

Training Activity (AFETA), under the Department of Defense. Afterwards, she was assigned to Langley Air Force Base, where she received additional training. She had been promoted swiftly up the ranks, as can happen to talented people in times of war.

Charlie was not squeamish. When a job had to be done, she could do it. The situation was life-and-death out here. She had sanctioned people and she had a good cover. She was young, pretty, and had an ample figure. No one would ever suspect she was an assassin. But because of things in her past, she found killing the bad people was not too much of a challenge. She got her orders, did what she was told and then moved on.

After all, it was war.

Then she met Bill Treese, and all six-foot-plus of him. He, his PBR or Patrol Boat River, Mark II, and his merry crew. A good-natured lot of them. They were young and tough, all hoping to be in a firefight every night, except Bill. He had a cool head about him.

They met while she was touring the base and being shown the Riverine Boats. Bill was swabbing the deck, shirtless, and had his fatigues rolled up past his knees to keep the soapy water off his uniform. As they were introduced by the Base Commander, they both felt an instant attraction.

Bill was big, muscular and burly, and looked born to command. Charlie liked strong men. For his part, other than the fact he had not seen a woman, let alone a female officer for over six months, (unless you counted the WAVE nurses, who only hung out with the doctors). Bill was also impressed with Charlie. She really was beautiful. He took a quick glance at her, wearing her fatigues. He could read a woman's body, like he could a boat's running lines.

She was taught and firm, with very nice superstructure in front, not so well hidden by her uniform.

"Nice boat," she said. "But why is the Commander swabbing the deck?"

Bill smiled, "I like it done a certain way. Too wet, and you can slip. Too dry, and it won't get clean. Plus, my Navy crew are off playing football against the Air Force guys. They're a bunch of wussies. By the way, I've never seen a uniform like that. What Branch are you serving in?"

"Air Force."

Bill rolled his eyes, "Oh, jeez! Sorry. Not all Air Force guys are wussies!"

The Base Commander, a Navy Captain, said, "You sure know how to make a great first impression, sailor!" They all laughed. "I need to get back. You two have a good time."

They both saluted the Captain.

"Permission to come aboard and look around?"

"Absolutely." They talked for the next two hours and over the next month, became friends and, when they could, clandestine lovers.

One day, Bill was alerted about a rescue mission in the jungle, upriver. Charlie was also told about it, and when she was asked if she would volunteer to go on the mission with him to bring back some wounded soldiers who had escaped the VC, plus several children from a village that had been gutted by air raids, she didn't hesitate to say yes.

The only bad thing was that Bill had only been given bare minimum, skeleton orders and not the complete story of the evacuation.

Charlie came from a military background. She had enlisted in the Air Force at 18, went to Officer Candidate School based on her tests, and was sent to flight school immediately. Soon she was flying jets and taking out North Vietnamese bridges and supply boats, when the CIA contacted her and asked her to interview for clandestine operations. They liked her because she was smart, brave and spoke fluent Vietnamese. As a fluke, when Charlie was very young, the family housekeeper was from Da Nang and it amused her to speak her native language to the little girl who was so bright, and said everything back to her in perfect dialect. This went on for years.

For the CIA, she had completed several missions. At some point, she realized she had become a spy; but not like someone who does good things to help her country, rather, like someone who does bad things, wrapped up in the flag of freedom.

She wasn't happy. She felt like she could be more helpful in the air than on the ground.

But she was committed to the CIA for the time being. She had decided she would rather go back to flying, and the CIA kept promising her they would give her a transfer back. Finally, this was her last mission. She had been given her orders to return to Travis Air Force Base in California, to start training as an instructor to teach other fighter pilots.

Bill came to her at the base the morning before his mission, when she was having breakfast and coffee. He smiled and shook her hand formally, even though they had been lovers, and had gotten very close over the past several weeks.

"I hear you may want to go with us on a fishing expedition," he said good-naturedly.

She smiled. "Sure, what are you fishing for?"

He smiled in return, but the smile never touched his eyes. "Souls. Lost and wounded souls. There was a firefight, but we cannot leave until tomorrow at 0200 hours. I have the general coordinates, and you have the precise coordinates. Our people were helping to rescue the children; most of the adults in the village were blown away. The kids were staying in bunkers built by the Viet Cong, and most of them made it out."

She looked down at her scrambled eggs, spam and toast. She had lost her appetite. "See you on board," she said softly.

Charlie made preparations all that day. She had her normal side arm service pistol and also several weapons, which she could not reveal, even to Bill Treese. Most of these things made a big bang, but she also had her sharp shooter rifle, which folded down to approximately the size of a briefcase. The rifle had a clip of 20 rounds, and a powerful scope, which attached to it. She could set it up and beak it down in less than 15 seconds. She had an extra 10 magazines, with ammo already loaded.

She also had several M18A1 Claymore Mines, which she could place in ambush positions, should there be a need to retreat against a hostile enemy. She could place one Claymore on the ground facing the pursuers and detonate it by remote control. The Claymore would fire a pattern of steel balls like a shotgun, directly into the kill zone. The balls would shoot out at 3,995 feet-per-second, to as much as 75 meters within a 60-degree arc, neutralizing most of the enemy. Modifications had been made so there was no detonation wire, meaning, you simply placed the weapon aiming behind you, (or in front, of you, depending on the situation), depress the detonation trigger, and get out of the way.

Charlie also had several C-4 explosive devices, much more powerful than the Claymore, which had to be handled extremely carefully. While they were relatively stable, the plastic explosives were packaged as M112 demolition blocks, weighing around 1.25 lbs. each, along with blasting caps for detonation. She carried a dozen of them, which would be used, if needed, either to destroy larger structures, or to booby-trap a squad of V.C.

She also had two MAC-10's; .45 ACP full auto machine pistols, which fired a 30-round magazine at 1,145 rounds per minute. The MAC stood for Military Armament Company, and was designed in 1964. Charlie had also taped two magazines end-on-end, so she simply had to eject the first magazine and turn it over, to be ready to fire immediately again. Because of her strength, she could fire both weapons simultaneously, effectively penetrating a small area with fire at a single target, or laying down spray fire for charging or retreating troops. She had several clips set up in the same manner.

Like Charlie, Bill Treese was also making preparations. Bill's River Patrol Boat was known as a Mark II riverine boat, or also known as a brown water boat, because it was used in the shallow, muddy water of the Viet Nam rivers. His was unusual, because it was on the larger side at 60 feet long and weighed in at 60 tons. It had guns, cannons and grenade launchers, but no metal armor, which helped with speed, but did not offer protection from the enemy.

Bill Treese was the Captain and made all the major decisions. His command and authority was absolute at all times. His Gunner's Mate was James, who operated all the weapons. His engine man, Tinker, was in charge of all of the engines and kept the boat running, no matter what. Lastly, his Patrol Officer, Dalton, was in charge of whatever mission they were on. He could also drive the boat and lend a hand with the firing of the weapons, if need be. Bill trusted all of these men with his life, especially Dalton, who was only two years younger than he, and had seen more than his share of action on the Mekong Delta.

An extra hand for the mission was a second gunner's mate, Tony, a good-natured Italian fellow from the Bronx in New York. He was a mechanic, who had found himself about to be drafted into the Army as a grunt, when he ran to the Navy recruiters and asked for sea duty. Hoping to be placed on a nice, big Aircraft Carrier, he had wound up instead on the rivers of South Viet Nam. In his mind, though, it could have been worse - so he made the best of the situation every day.

Bill looked out at the dock, which was loaded with munitions. Dalton had a thick clipboard, on which he was checking off everything that was being loaded onboard, weapons, food, water, fuel and everything else they would need. There was even an extra-thick mosquito net, procured from a late-night poker game. Dalton, smiled. Even in Southeast Asia, there were rewards for a man who knew how to play cards.

"Do we have everything?" Bill inquired of Dalton.

"Yes, Captain," Dalton turned and saluted him.

"No need to be formal," Bill replied with a smile. "We need to get off this dock in a few hours, and I want to have everything loaded and lashed down. How about the ordnance? It could get messy up there. They really haven't told me much."

"Pretty much everything is on-board. Even extra peanut butter."

Bill rolled his eyes. "That's the best we can hope to eat?

Supposed to be a two-day mission!"

Dalton smiled. "The PB is for the kids, along with bread, honey, jam and some cereal. I've got fish, chicken and some steaks for us, that we can pan-fry pretty quickly. Plus, coffee. Lots of coffee."

"OK. That's perfect. Do we have extra medical supplies, in case there are more wounded than we were led to believe?"

"Yeah," said Dalton. "It cost me a case of chocolate bars, but I got the medics to cough me up a bunch of bandages and meds. So, we're all right."

"It would be nice to know the whole mission," grumbled Bill.

Dalton was looking over Bill's left shoulder at a shadowy figure approaching the boat. "Well," he said, "you might want to ask her," motioning with his chin towards the figure.

Bill turned, just as Charlie appeared in the low-level light of the dock. She was carrying what looked to be a very heavy backpack, which was camouflaged. It was strapped to her shoulders, extended down to the back of her thighs, and was supported by a thick belt around her waist. She saluted Bill.

"Permission to come aboard, Sir?"

Bill saluted back. "Permission granted."

As she started up the gangplank, Bill reached out his hand to steady her as she climbed aboard. As their hands touched, their eyes locked on each other.

There was a moment of awkward silence.

"Well," started Bill, "you come prepared. May I ask what you have brought on board my vessel?"

"You may ask," Charlie's eyes twinkled a bit, at the joke. Then she continued, "But some of this stuff is that secret military shit,

that I'm not supposed to talk about... With all due respect, Sir"
she added hastily.

Bill thought for a minute. Technically speaking, they were
both Captains, he in the Navy, and she in the Air Force. But this
was his boat, and he had a right to know what was being brought
on-board his vessel.

Not wanting to push it, he decided to play his part well, even
though they were both too smart to believe he was that naive.
"Okay. We'll let it go at that. It's not my nature to look up a lady's
knickers, but, of course, I am responsible for the lives and safety of
my crew and boat. So, let me ask you again. Anything dangerous
in that back pack?"

Charlie nodded slowly, afraid to hear what his next question
would be.

"Is it dangerous for the enemy, or for me?"

"Definitely for the enemy, Sir! Again, with all due respect, I
have been sent not only to help your and my mission, but to add
physical support as well. Technically, when we discuss the mission
in detail, once we are underway, my job is to provide guidance to
the target and to support your flank, as we move in and out. But,
that's all I'm at liberty to say at this time, Sir."

Bill nodded. He looked at his watch. "Okay. We'll leave in
about six hours. You can store your gear below decks in the X-O's
quarters. He'll bunk with the crew. It's really tight down there, but
we won't be onboard this tub for more than a few days. Maybe
you can get a little sleep. It's hot; I know that. So, if you want to
sleep on the deck, we have mosquito netting available. Whatever
you want. Savvy?"

She nodded gratefully at his reasonableness, and at the

opportunity to get a little shut-eye. "Yes, Sir!" she said.

Bill held up his hand. "One more thing. I don't out-rank you, so please call me Bill, or Captain Treese. Sir is not a term I'm used to dealing with out here."

Charlie smiled at him, thinking that there were a lot of cute things she could call him if the crew were not around. But now they were on a mission, and all missions were inherently dangerous when you went into hostile territory. There was no time for anything, especially thoughts or discussions about their personal lives.

She turned to walk down the ladder below deck. Almost against his will, Bill couldn't help but follow her backside with his eyes. He shook it off. Not a good idea to look at her that way on a mission. Need to focus, or they all might get sent back home in body bags.

****

The boat got underway at precisely 0200. The water was calm, but the atmosphere was hot and oppressive, even at this early-morning hour. It was dark, as they moved upriver at a steady 24 knots. They had done what they could to muffle the loud riverine engines for a night approach.

Charlie had briefed Bill and Dalton, his Patrol Officer. The rest of the crew would be filled in when they got closer to their target.

"So, we will be arriving just before dawn in about three-and-a-half hours at our current speed," said Charlie. "Our mission is to collect approximately 12 children, four South Vietnamese adults and four wounded American soldiers. Everyone is mobile and can walk. I don't think they can run, but when we get there, we will find out."

"Who did the recon?" asked Bill.

"Two guys who directed in the helicopter and then were taken captive by the V.C. We don't know what happened to them, but the pilot doesn't think he was spotted."

She pulled out a rough map, and they all studied it carefully.

"The camp and what is left of the village are here, about a click from the river. There are small hills to the right and a deep jungle to the left. There are several bends to the trail, which can be blind ambush spots for the V.C.

"The plan is for me to take you both as close as we can to the village, and then break off to cover your flank from the series of hills all the way back to the boat; and then get away, right as dawn is hitting, back to the base."

Bill thought for a minute and was quiet. He didn't know anything about Charlie's battle skills, and had no idea if she could cover their escape, or even get them to the village. He knew she was technically in charge of this operation, but he was in the dark about her experience and expertise. Because of that, he chose his words carefully.

He smiled at her. "Are you a good shot?" he asked.

"Yes," was her curt response.

He looked at Dalton and their eyes met. Bill continued, "With all due respect, it would seem they would have sent more men and," he stumbled a little, "more women?"

Charlie had been through this before. "You'll have to trust me on this. I was the best they had when the mission was decided."

"Trust has to be earned," said Dalton, looking squarely at her. "Sir!"

Bill nodded. "Especially in matters of life and death. Plus, the lives of these kids, troops and civilians - who, by the way, could be V.C. in disguise. They could get us back to the boat and incinerate us!"

Charlie nodded. "I anticipated your concerns. I have brought a few things to mitigate the situation in our favor."

Bill was not easily placated. "Ok. Well, we have our orders, so we will do whatever it takes to see this thing through. One thing, though, I do want to bring an extra man. Our Junior Gunnery Mate, Tony, is tough as nails and can think well on his feet. We will take the four of us, and leave James and Tinker on- board to help us with our escape. Plus, Tony has a lot of experience as a medic. That was his job before his boat was shot out from under him last month."

Charlie thought about this. It made sense. "Ok, I agree. Let me give you the coordinates."

The pilot who had given Headquarters the info about the village had been right about a lot of things, but one thing he was dead wrong about, was the fact that he had been spotted. Just after the Viet Cong troops took the two American soldiers prisoner, they spotted his Iroquois Helicopter as he turned and dropped over the hills. He was sitting on the ground now, in the darkness on the other side of the hills Charlie had mentioned. His Co-pilot, Crew Chief and Door Gunner were all sacked out in the back. Once the rescue crew made contact with him, he had to supply air support if needed, or possibly extract one or more members of the party. He glanced uneasily at his radio, as if it might go off any second.

****

The North Viet Cong soldiers were gathering. They had kept these babies alive, as well as the old ones, and the wounded troops to use as hostages. They knew the Americans would come. Maybe for the villagers, probably for their brothers-in-arms, but definitely for the babies. Americans were so soft!

The commander looked over the mostly destroyed village. He could make out the sleeping figures in the open square. He could just make this whole thing easier by telling his troops to just kill them all while they slept, but he had his orders. When the Americans came, they would gather them all up, the hostages would think they were safe and then, when the Americans led them out, they would then kill them all. He didn't know how many there would be, but because they saw the helicopter and because the two prisoners had told them very little, except that there would be a rescue attempt the next day. So, he had been given three dozen troops, in addition to his own 10 staked out around the village. The rest he had positioned in the jungle with a few on the hill directly overlooking the village. He cocked his automatic machine gun and waited in the dark.

The Riverine boat cut her engines 100 feet from shore and glided into an overgrown blind, directed by Charlie. She, Bill, Dalton and Tony wore jungle fatigues, heavy facial paint and thick boots. They each had several weapons, as well as machetes for close combat, and to kill snakes in the jungle. Charlie also had her backpack and Tony carried a backpack full of medical supplies and extra ammo.

As the boat touched the shore, Dalton jumped on-shore and, taking the towline in hand, pulled the boat under a large overgrowth of thick bushes and tied it off.

Bill, Charlie and Tony jumped off and joined him on shore. It was still the better part of dark as they moved away from the boat. Both James and Tinker were manning the weapons on-deck, with Tinker taking a quick break to keep checking the engines, which were at idle. He had to keep everything hot in order to make a fast escape, but not run low on fuel, either. This mission was not supposed to take very long.

Quietly they moved along the jungle path, with Charlie on point and Bill in the rear. After about 300 yards, Charlie stopped suddenly in the gloom and raised her hand. Bill and the others, moved forward quietly to join her. She pointed to a trip wire strung tightly across the path. She pointed down, and shook her head, raising two fingers, indicating that there were probably two more ahead of this one.

They stepped carefully over the wire and, sure enough, spotted two more trip wires ahead on the trail 10 feet apart, that they stepped over as well. Tony, pulled out a can of fluorescent orange spray paint and sprayed all three wires, so that they could see them when they returned to the boat with the hostages. Bill smiled and whispered, to Tony, "Just like spraying graffiti on the overpasses in the Bronx?" he asked, as his eyes twinkled. Tony looked away with his nose in the air, pretending to be insulted. Charlie motioned for them to move ahead in standard order.

As they had moved in just under one click, by their estimation, they rounded a bend and spotted what was left of the destroyed village. Charlie motioned for Bill to move forward next to her.

They crouched down, and she whispered to all of them, "The village is there. The kids are sleeping out in the open. The troops and the adult villagers could be anywhere. But the children are the priority."

Bill nodded, but he knew he wouldn't leave anyone behind if he could help it.

He looked at her. She pointed to her chest and indicated she was going to move out to the hills on their right.

He nodded. "How long do you need?" he asked.

"I need 17 minutes, exactly. Move closer to the target!"

Bill nodded again. He looked toward the village, then turned back to ask Charlie one more question, but she had disappeared into the jungle.

He set the timer on his watch, and he and his crew moved in closer. Just behind a small berm of rock and dirt, likely created by the last bombing run by the V.C., they peered over and looked at the open square in front of the destroyed buildings.

It was getting a little lighter, and they could see many sleeping figures. Bill motioned for them to wait.

Charlie had taken off, but not toward the hills. Not yet. She ran backwards toward the boat, and planted four Claymore mines along the trail, with the detonating force to blow back toward the village, cutting off any hostile pursuers. She then dashed across toward the hills and, on her way up, placed two C-4 charges with blasting clips at the base of two of the hills where she would be doing recon, protecting their flank.

As she got to Bluff Number Two, which was closer to the river than to the village, she spotted two V.C. troops looking away from her, toward the village. She holstered her weapon, pulled out her Ka-Bar Military knife, and crept up behind them. It was over quickly, without a struggle. She dragged their bodies behind a clump of rocks and left them there with their rifles, grabbed their hand grenades and clipped them onto her belt.

She moved forward quickly to the next hilltop, named Bluff Number One. Now there was a problem. There were four V.C. troops looking over the village, out of sight from below. She suddenly realized they were heading into an ambush - and there was nothing she could do!

Bill looked at his watch. At the seventeen-minute mark, they moved out. Light was beginning to flood the village. They could see people sleeping under rough covers to protect them from the moist air. It was still hot, but not oppressively so.

It looked like a slam-dunk. No one was around. He and Dalton moved forward. Tony stayed behind to protect the rear from any potential ambush.

Bill approached the first figure cautiously. He bent down and touched a child's hair. It was a young boy. He shook him gently. The boy turned over on his back and opened his eyes. He saw Bill and started to yell in surprise, but Bill placed his left hand over the child's mouth and, with his other hand brought the first finger up to his lips in the universal gesture to be silent. The boy closed his eyes for a second, nodding his head in agreement.

Dalton, meanwhile, was doing the same with the others. Eventually he and Bill had aroused the rest of the sleeping kids, the four adult villagers and the four wounded Americans.

Bill went up to one of the soldiers, who was holding his right side as he lay on the ground. "Can you guys move out ok?"

The soldier nodded. "Yes, sir. We can all move. How far?"

"Just one click to the..." he said; suddenly they were surrounded by 8 V. C. soldiers, with their weapons drawn. One soldier who was speaking in rapid Vietnamese, motioned violently towards Bill.

The wounded American spoke again. "Drop your weapons, he said."

On Bluff Number One, Charlie carefully made her way closer to the four V.C. troops who were no longer crouching, but were looking over the hill toward the village. After hearing loud talking both from down below and up here on top, she knew their mission had been blown. Carefully, she opened three C-4 explosives and placed blasting caps into the soft plastic. She moved silently towards the four troops; whose attention was captured by the action that was taking place down below. After she placed them under a large stacked group of rocks between her and the guards, she fell back and waited.

Bill and Dalton were on their knees, with their feet crossed, and their hands behind their heads. The Viet Cong Officer in charge was speaking in rapid loud language to the wounded soldier.

"He says you are spies and so are not subject to the Geneva Convention or any mercy, for that matter. He is going to shoot you both first, and then the rest of us."

Bill glanced at Dalton and said to the soldier, "Tell him he can kiss my ever-lovin' ass!"

Instead of waiting for the translation, the angry Commander strode up to Bill and, using the butt of his rifle, struck him in the back of the head, which only dazed Bill, but did not knock him out. He fell forward and lay there in the soft dirt.

Tony, from the back, had been watching all of this take place. Just as he raised his rifle to fire on the Commander, a rifle barrel was placed against his cheek. He glanced up at the V.C. soldier and dropped his weapon.

Tony was marched into the clearing by the soldier who had captured him. Alarmed, the Commander, angry that he had almost been ambushed, strode over to Tony and the soldier and hit Tony in his mid-section with the butt of his rifle. Tony let out a loud "Whoosh," and fell to the ground, doubled over.

The Commander raised his rifle in the air high over Tony's head, about to smash in his skull with the butt of his rifle. He held still for a minute, getting a better aim.

Charlie had scrambled back, but she knew she was close, and could be either injured or killed by the C-4. There was no guarantee. "What the hell," she thought as she pressed the command detonator and ducked down.

Just as the V.C. Commander started to bring the butt of his rifle down onto Tony's head, there was suddenly a tremendous explosion on the hill up and to the left. Rocks shot a thousand feet into the air, and then rained down. The whole hillside began to slide down in a huge avalanche, carrying the bodies of the V.C soldiers with it.

As the other V.C. soldiers watched in disbelief, Bill and Dalton jumped up and grabbed their weapons. They turned them on the V.C. soldiers who had been guarding them and, without hesitation, executed them. The Commander had been knocked off his feet and was struggling to get up, but a large rock had grazed his head. As he reached for his rifle, Tony, who had gained his footing, kicked the Commander savagely in the head across his temple, effectively killing him instantly.

On what was left of Bluff Number One, Charlie had been blown back by the blast. Dazed, she recovered and jumped to her feet. Her only option was to retreat to Bluff Number Two, as there was little left of Bluff Number One. She moved quickly to Bluff Number Two and looked out. She could hear loud noises behind her beyond the bluff, away from the trail. That could only mean VC soldiers beyond the hill were descending on her position.

Suddenly, as she looked across the trail they would be escaping on, she heard the same loud noises of troop movement coming right toward them. She pulled out her radio. "Fleece," she screamed into the mike, "this is Sheep. Get out, out, out now!!! Hostilities on the move. Going towards the trail!"

Bill heard his radio crackle to life; Charlie's words to get out made him spring into action.

"Dalton, Tony, move out! It's now or never. Get the kids and everyone else. Now, now, now!!!"

Tony and Dalton sprang into action, grabbing the kids and the adults out of their crouched positions. They all broke for the trail, with Dalton in the lead, Tony in the middle, and Bill at the end. The kids were trying to move fast, past Dalton, but he held them back. The old Vietnamese villagers and the wounded U.S. soldiers were struggling, but keeping up as best as they could. When they rounded the second large curve, they saw the V.C. soldiers coming out of the jungle canopy to their right.

There were roughly a dozen soldiers who were running straight at them. These V.C. soldiers had orders to try to capture the Americans alive as hostages and bargaining chips for their captured comrades, but to execute them all, if all else failed.

Seeing their prey, they began to charge, holding their rifles up, taking aim.

Charlie had regained the top of Bluff Number Two, just in time to see the V.C. soldiers emerge from the jungle on the other side of the trail and begin to charge Bill and his group.

She waited for what seemed like an eternity. Two of the V.C. soldiers who had broken away from the rest and were charging hard towards Bills group and were about to fire. Unfortunately, Bill was not past the first claymore yet.

Charlie reached into her backpack and pulled out her sharpshooter rifle. In a few seconds, she had it set up and positioned, took aim and, firing quickly and accurately, dropped the first two enemy soldiers. By then, Bill's group had cleared the mines she had set. As the V.C. soldiers charged past the bodies of their two comrades, and took aim at the fleeing group, Charlie depressed the firing pin of the Claymore.

A gigantic explosion was heard, with thousands of steel balls firing back at, and into the bodies of the pursuing V.C. soldiers.

Not one of them survived

Knocked to the ground by the shock wave, along with several of the adults, Bill looked back to see that his pursuers were all dead. He jumped up and, looking back to his left, saw the figure of a girl on Bluff Number Two, jumping off the hill and running down towards the trail. What he didn't see was over two dozen V.C. soldiers ascending the bluff from the other side, and Charlie running for her life.

Bill jumped up and commanded everyone to keep moving toward the river. Suddenly, once again there were shouts coming from the jungle on his right, and he knew that more V.C. troops were pursuing them. He didn't know that Charlie, running toward him on his left flank, also knew they were there, and, just as she had done before, once Bill and his group passed safely, she pressed the trigger while on the run. The Claymore exploded and shot steel balls through the oncoming V.C. soldiers. Again, there were no survivors.

Winded, tired, but still full of adrenaline, Bill could not help but smile as he raced ahead. *That girl has real balls,* he thought. *We would all be dead without her!*

There was only about a quarter of a click's worth of time to get to the boat, where they might be duck soup for any sitting V.C. snipers or other marksmen hiding in the jungle. Experts that they were, the snipers wouldn't make noise like the first troops did. They would just silently shoot the crew dead before they had even reached the boat.

Just as he had that thought, a bullet whisked past his right ear and exploded harmlessly onto a tree trunk in front of him. Suddenly, bullets began to rain down on them from what seemed like everywhere. Bill lurched forward to try to cover up the children, but the adults were in the way. Somehow, they all managed to evade the bullets.

Once again, Charlie had planned for this. She could not call in an airstrike to knock these guys out, because it was too close to Bill and the kids. So she had planted more C-4s in the woods around the trail. She was watching as Bill and his group rounded the last corner, moving to their left to get to the riverine boat.

Suddenly, Bill heard the two dozen V.C. soldiers running down Bluff Number Two on his left. There was no sign of Charlie. The soldiers from the jungle on his right had been neutralized, but they were under fire from snipers, to the left and behind them, probably in the trees. As they rounded the last bend, he could see the boat tied up to the shore.

"Run!" Bill shouted at his group. And, while most did not speak English, they instinctively made a charge for the relative safety of the boat.

On the boat, James and Tinker had been under fire from the snipers for the past few minutes, and, while they were cautions because they didn't know where Bill and the others were, they managed to get off a few bursts of fire in the direction of the enemy rifle sounds form the deck-mounted machine guns.

They saw Bill, the children and the rest, running and lurching for the boat and knew they had little time. Tinker leaped up from his firing position, jumped overboard to the shore and started pushing the heavy boat out into the water, which allowed for a faster escape, but also made it a more visible target for enemy fire. As the momentum pushed the boat out away from the shore, he jumped back aboard and, running below decks to the engine room, began firing up the engines - all while James continued to lay down fire over the heads of Bill's group.

Bullets rained down, and as they reached the boat, they had to splash through a couple of feet of water to get onboard. Dalton, in the lead, grabbed the kids and slung them up into the arms of James, who had abandoned his weapon for the time being.

"Tony!" shouted Bill, "Get up there and help him!" Tony moved up and began to throw the kids onboard and help the villagers and wounded troops aboard as well.

Bill turned around and, raising his machine gun, started firing at the trees in a wild scatter. Even if he did not hit the snipers, the shock of the return fire might slow them down.

Just then, he thought about Charlie. Where was she? He glanced down at the trail, but did not see her. Just as he was about to resume firing, his radio crackled to life.

"Fire in the hole! Get out , out, out!!!!"

Bill jumped on-board. The kids, the troopers and the villagers had gone below to hide. Bill ran back to the throttle and jammed the boat in reverse, at full throttle.

Charlie had been watching this from her position on the side of the trail near the jungle and away from the bluffs. She saw the descending V.C. from the Bluffs. Though she had another Claymore in position, it was too late, as they were past the line of fire. She heard the snipers, but could not see them. When she looked at Bill's boat, that's when she saw the last of the group being hoisted aboard and Bill shooting blindly into the treetops. That's when she called him on the radio immediately. As the boat moved back, she knew it would be close.

Pulling out the last C-4 detonator, she pushed the button.

The explosion shot flames hundreds of feet in the air, and the shock wave rocked the heavy riverine boat as Bill and the others on deck were flattened out. Charlie herself, in spite of ducking down behind a dirt berm and several palm trees, felt herself being flung backwards, hitting her head against a large rock. Only her helmet protected her, and kept her from losing consciousness. The explosion kept going and, because the now-dead V.C. soldiers had weapons, their ordinance began lighting off, setting off a series of explosions.

Charlie, wounded and dazed, started running for the boat. There was still the roar and aftershock of the explosion all around her, but more aftershocks on the other side of the trail nearer the bluffs, or at least, what was left of them.

She splashed through the water, and as she tried to jump up on-board was met by Bill leaning over the side; his two strong hands grabbing her arms and hoisted her on-board.

"You OK?" he asked, concern written all over his face. Charlie just lay on the deck, panting. Finally, she looked up at him.

"Yes, I...I... think so." She shivered in spite of the heat, and Bill wrapped his arms around her.

"Thanks for saving our lives," he said. "What else you got in that purse of yours, or should I ask?"

"No, you should *not* ask, and you're welcome!"

They both looked at the carnage in the jungle. Smoke and fire were everywhere, and, while it was not a raging inferno and would burn itself out, but it would leave a permanent mark on the jungle canopy. As they looked out, Dalton came up on deck.

"One of the old villagers said something about a baby being left behind."

Charlie said, "Bring her up here at once!"

Dalton hastily retreated and within a few seconds, had the woman, who looked to be about 70, and was old, wrinkled, and frail, was on the deck. She sat down heavily. Charlie and Bill kneeled next to her.

She was speaking excitedly in Vietnamese, and Charlie was listening intently. Every once in a while, she said something to the old lady, who nodded and answered back.

After a minute, Charlie stood up. "I have to go back."

"What?" said Bill, "Why?"

"There is a child back at the village who was trapped in the wreckage; they forgot about her in all the excitement. I have to go back and get her."

"No," said Bill. "We cannot risk the others. We need to get out of here! That's an order!"

Charlie grabbed her backpack and pulled out the two Mack 10's. She reached into her backpack again and pulled out two long magazines for them. In fact, there were actually a total of ten magazines, two taped end-to-end, for a total of 60 automatic rounds-per-magazine. When they emptied the first magazines, they simply ejected the spent clip and turned over to the other side to shoot the second clip.

She slung the backpack over her shoulders, held her Mac 10's in both hands and smiled at Bill.

"You're welcome to come, or you can stay here, but I'm going." With that, she jumped over the side and splashed to the shore.

"Shit!" Bill yelled. He turned to Dalton. "If were not back in 20 minutes, or you're under fire, get the hell out of here. In the meantime, go back down river a couple of clicks and wait for me to call!"

"Aye, aye, sir!" was Dalton's response, plus a smart salute, out of respect.

Bill grabbed his machine gun and jumped into the water, which was now almost up to his waist. He splashed to the shore and took off after Charlie.

Charlie had run about half of the distance to the village, when she felt compelled to stop and wait for Bill, who she knew was laboriously running after her. So she squatted on the side of the trail behind a tree.

She looked around her. It was full early morning now, and

the sun was coming up. This was an ugly sight. Like any other battlefield, the dead were strewn around amidst plenty of blood. The Claymores had done their job on the jungle side of the trail, and the C-4 and the Claymores had done their job for the rest on the bluff side. At the moment, there were no apparent survivors or any threat from the enemy.

She heard Bill wheezing and running up to her position before she saw him. He plopped down next to her, breathing hard.

"Jeez, you can run," he said, sweat pouring off his brow and re-staining his shirt.

"What kept you?" was her smart reply.

Bill looked around. "Traffic."

She smiled. "I think we're safe to proceed to the…..," her voice was drowned out by automatic fire from both sides of the trail, to the front of them, and also behind them.

"Oops. Spoke too soon!"

They both ducked down as the scatter-fire searched for them on the trail.

Bill spoke first, "This is suicide!"

Charlie said, "Yes. But you can go back."

"Hell, no. The safest place is beside you! Who goes first?"

Charlie solved the problem by jumping up and taking off toward the village down the trail. Bill rolled his eyes, but chased after her.

Charlie shot both Mac 10 guns so that the right-hand gun faced her right side and her left-hand gun faced her left side, with barrels extended so that the expended shells would eject harmlessly away from her.

She opened up, guns blazing on both sides as she ran up the

trail. Bill, running behind her, saw the muzzle flash and the report of gunfire straight ahead and up on a wide berm in front of them. He fired off three rounds above Charlie's head. Unlike Charlie, firing at full auto, Bill's M2 carbine was set to fire three bullet bursts, which helped him aim better each time. The result was that the forward attackers, between them and the village, were shut down in a few seconds. Charlie also found success, as the V.C. soldiers who were not killed by her initial run up the trail, when she was firing on both sides, fell back and hid in the trees.

After running for five more minutes, they reached the village.

"The village lady said to look for the house that is destroyed, but has one front window still intact on the left side," said Charlie.

"Left side facing us, or left side looking backwards?" asked Bill.

Charlie shot him a look full of daggers, as Bill shrugged his shoulders.

Fortunately, the hut was right in front of them. As they passed it, Bill looked down at the soldiers they had shot earlier, just to make sure they were dead.

Against all caution, Charlie ran to the window that had no glass, peered in for a second and, to Bill's horror, dived in.

Bill ran to the hut. "Charlie?"

"Here. Coming out!" She emerged from the window, with a baby wrapped in her arms.

Bill looked at the child, who was wrapped in a rough, old army blanket up to her chin. She was dark and her eyes blazed out at Bill and the world, although she uttered no sounds. "She's hot," said Charlie. "I think she has a fever."

Before Bill could react, suddenly bullets were flying all around them. They dove under the canopy of the bombed-out hut and instinctively rolled under the collapsed portion. It would help for a minute or two, but they both knew they were sitting ducks.

Bill spoke first, above the roar of the automatic gunfire. "Love to hear any ideas you might have for getting out of this."

Charlie was behind him, holding the baby. Bill had his back pressed into her and he could feel the heat coming off of the infant. *Geez,* he thought. *I either get to die from bullets, or from whatever disease this kid has.*

He could feel Charlie pulling something out of her backpack.

"Tango, Whisky, Tango," she then whispered into her radio. "Need extraction, point Delta."

"As planned," she added. They heard static on her radio and then a very faint, "Roger."

"What was that?" asked Bill.

"My idea. You asked my idea, so we're getting out via helicopter."

"Ok, but what about them?" asked Bill.

"May be a problem," she paused. "Or maybe not."

She spoke into the radio again. "Black cloud. Seagate here. Forever drop on my command, one half-click beyond coordinates five, niner, niner, niner, four. Copy?"

The radio cracked to life, "Roger that, Seagate. Five, niner, niner, niner, four. Here comes the music!"

"What the fuck?" said Bill.

"Better tell your boat to get the hell out of here," said Charlie. "It's going to get really hot in a minute."

Bill grabbed his radio. "PBR II. Get out now! Extraction point, Abort, abort, abort! Get to the landing place Bravo Two.

Now! Now! Now!"

Suddenly, they heard the sound of the madly spinning rotaries of the UH-1B Iroquois Helicopter swooping in over the village.

Charlie's radio screamed to life. "We're out of here now. Under heavy fire!"

Charlie pushed Bill forward and jumped over him, while at the same time shoving the baby into his arms. Bill stood up and backed into the wall of the hut as Charlie raced into the middle of the village square. She yelled at him to hit the deck. Bill flattened out onto the ground.

There were bullet tracings all around Charlie as she first started firing her Mac 10's in a 360-degree circle all around her, while moving from side to side. As the fire around her slowed down somewhat, she jumped back towards the hut and started heaving the enemy grenades she had captured earlier into all random directions. Explosions rained out all around them, almost stopping all of the enemy fire. Suddenly, the helicopter came into sight and hovered over the village square where Charlie had stood a minute before.

She screamed at Bill above the roar of the blades, "Let's go!"

Bill clung tightly to the baby, raced across the square , and dove headfirst into the chopper's open hatch. Charlie, still holding and firing her weapons, dove in after them. The crew chief grabbed all three of them and secured them with safety lines.

"Out, Tommy," she screamed at the pilot, "The music is coming! The music is coming! Get us the hell out of here!"

The pilot nodded and pulled the Iroquois up on a steep bank. Suddenly several bullets punctured the fabric of the helicopter's sides. Black smoke started to pour out of the bullet holes, but the captain, checking his instruments, shouted out they were ok, even as he suddenly spun the helicopter around and slipped it sideways and down several feet to avoid tracer fire coming at them from the right.

The pilot started again pulling up again after his maneuver trying to get out of range. That's when they saw the F-4 Phantom jet screaming in, dropping napalm all over the village and the surrounding jungle. Everything became incinerated as the fiery mushroom cloud enveloped the entire village including the surrounding jungle and bluffs, wiping everything out. The fire rose to the base of the helicopter, threatening to pull it down in its heat as it created a downdraft.

Onboard the helicopter, Bill had been holding the child, whose intense body heat had been burning through his Navy camouflage fatigues. He took a minute to look down at her, expecting to see the sweet innocence of a child, but instead, the burning, intense eyes of a demon stared straight back at him.

Bill gasped and set the baby down, on the deck, even as the helicopter, began to spin and yaw as a reaction to the explosions down below. It was as hot in the helicopter as it was outside! Bill stared at her and she back at him. He looked away frantically at what they had rescued, although his rational mind told him she was just a child who had been victimized and was in shock.

Just as the vessel tilted and spun to the left as the result of a violent explosion, the helicopter rotated on its side and threatened to go into a tailspin. The baby, lying by itself on the deck of the helicopter, had somehow become unsecured from her safety lanyard and began to slide toward the open hatch. She was about to fall out of the aircraft, directly into the fire below!

Bill never moved. He was paralyzed on the spot; every brain cell and every fabric in his being screamed at him to grab the infant and save her, but the muscles in his body would not move.

Suddenly the Iroquois helicopter lurched and spun counterclockwise and the infant was hurled out of the open hatch!

As if by magic, Charlie was there and, reaching out into the void, snatched the baby out of thin air and brought her back into the cargo bay of the helicopter.

She stared at Bill, both knowing what he had done - and also not done - to save the child. What was worse, the baby also stared accusingly at Bill.

As the chopper stabilized and began to set a course to meet the PBR boat and move back to base, Bill looked away into the distance.

The wind off Mt. Diablo had turned into a loud gale. The rain had given way to hail, and the thunder and lightning made it seem as if all Hell was breaking loose.

Charlie, looking off into the distance, sipped from her glass of brandy; the fiery liquid burned her throat. It was a most welcome sensation.

They had been taken downriver to their base camp. Bill had alerted his crew aboard the PBR to go back without them and return to base. Charlie and Bill did not speak to each other until the next day, when the Base Commander wanted to debrief them on what had happened and how a large section of Viet Nam was now barren, due to an unauthorized napalm attack.

That conversation had not gone well. Bill and Charlie, who were relieved of their commands, were ordered to face a military tribunal. Bill's situation was better than hers, mostly because he had been acting on orders and, unfortunately, had to tell them everything they had done.

Some things followed military protocol, but most of Charlie's actions did not, and she was scheduled for a General Court Martial. At the moment, she was under house arrest with the baby by her side the whole time, mostly because no one knew quite what to do with the baby.

While she was waiting for trial, one early morning, the Base Commander knocked at the tent pole outside her tent. He stuck his head inside and told her she would be moving out in 15 minutes, and to gather her things and also the baby girl. As they came outside, a large transport jeep with one gunnery jeep in front and also one behind showed up and whisked them off into the jungle.

She was allowed an Honorable Discharge and awarded custody of the girl. They flew for 24 hours on an Air Force jet back to Travis Air Force Base in California. There, the CIA and the military commanders then debriefed her. She was given her discharge papers and left the Service forever, moving in with family members in the San Francisco Bay Area. Although she thought about Bill Treese many times, she never saw him again.

Bill fared better. He was returned to his command, given a Commendation for Bravery and awarded the Navy Silver Star Medal for heroism in the line of duty for saving the wounded soldiers. Bill never wore that Silver Star, because he knew who the real hero was that day, and she had been kicked out of the Service for her heroism.

Charlie felt, rather than heard, her daughter's presence. She turned around to see her standing in the shadows.

"Don't worry about him," she said spitefully, then spat into her open palm, and punched it with the fist of her other hand. Zenadia looked at her mother and knew she was thinking about Bill Treese.

Charlie turned back to the window, took a long drink of brandy, and closed her eyes against the weather.

CHAPTER FOUR

ZENADIA

ZENADIA WAS NOT OF THIS WORLD. She had been born in the Amazon jungle to a mother who was considered a wild woman and a devil worshipper by the villagers. When they saw the woman near the river, upstream, always upstream, those who were Christians crossed themselves; those that were not, made the sign of the devil's hand. She was never approached and she never approached the villagers.

She lived in the jungle and always was humming or chanting, but no one knew what was the meaning of the music or words were.

One day she came to the river with an odd-looking bundle in her arms. It was small and didn't move, even when she bent down to retrieve water. It looked like a baby, but made no noise, ever. She came a half-dozen times over a couple of months, then was never seen alive again.

One day, two of the local men came back from their fishing

hunt and were talking excitedly to the village elders. They had found the body of the "wild woman" at the bottom of the large falls on the other side of the mountain, lying partially on the shore. Afraid to touch her, lest she leap up and put a curse on them, the men watched her for over an hour, half-in and half-out of the cold water, but she never moved and did not appear to be breathing.

There was no sign of the child.

The next day, several of the men and two of the women who were considered healers, went out to the site to see if they could figure out what had happened to her. They did not see her body, but found her clothes and jewels and so assumed she had been eaten by a predator. So they were not prepared for what they saw when they journeyed to the other side of the falls. On a flat rock, next to the river was the dead body of the woman tied to stakes by her hands and feet, wearing only tatters of her clothing.

The group stepped away after saying several prayers, both pagan and Christian, not just for her soul, but also for their own souls and, more importantly, for the protection of the village. As quickly as they could, they got away from her body and that evil place.

Her child was never seen or heard from again, and the villagers tried to forget about both of them forever.

Zenadia was that child and she was born "aware," meaning she knew things she should not have known about as a baby; that she was born to the wild woman and that there was no love, only a trust that both would survive. So, when the mist took her mother away to the falls and then came back and took her away, she had only a recollection that was as it was supposed to be.

Her next memory was of another jungle, hot and steamy.

There were loud noises all around her. She was underneath a great weight of plants and hard wood. Her mother grabbed her and brought her into a flying machine, which went into the air. She didn't know this as a fact, but she felt it.

There was a man on the flying machine who looked at her with fear. When they left the ground, she felt herself floating outside in the flames, which were not hot, but soothing. Their eyes met and he looked away, as she floated away into space. Suddenly, she felt strong hands on her body pulling her back into the flying machine. She looked at the man, who did not look at her again.

After that, her mother took care of her for many years. She knew she was different. She was never cold. She knew things. She knew what people were thinking, especially about her. That's why she could never go to school or have playmates. She was home-schooled and lived in virtual isolation with her mother, which suited her very well.

When they first came to the U.S., they lived with some of her mother's relatives. She didn't like it when her mother went to work and she had to be alone with the family all day. She didn't speak to them, and they didn't understand her. They fed her and made sure she was clean, but she never slept, even as an infant, until her mother came home. Then they would go to bed together. She would watch her, unblinking even then, until she heard her mother's rhythmic breathing as she fell asleep.

As she got a little older, her mother would read the newspapers, about the stock market. Her mother was investing her meager wages as a waitress in a local café, having never been able to fly again, due to her honorable military discharge. She also received a very small pension from the Service, which did not go far.

One day her mother pointed to two different stocks in the newspaper. "Which one should I buy, honey?"

Zenadia didn't hesitate. She pointed to the one with the name "Dark Royal."

Her mother invested $80.00, all the money she had. By the next day, the stock doubled. By the end of the week, it was up 200%, and then split, and split again. Her mother was going to sell, but Zenadia, shook her head and pointed to another stock she saw on the stock sheet, which said, "Black Horse." Her mother invested the same amount of $80.00, and the same thing happened. By then, she knew something uncanny was up, regarding her daughter's ability to predict great stock market investments.

It went on like that for over a year. By then, they were worth over two million dollars, and bought a nice house in the newer area of Danville, California, which was being developed. Over the next several years, they were able to buy more stocks and then diversify with bonds and entered the burgeoning real estate market of the region in the early 1980's. Many new developments were being built, and Zenadia, in spite of her youth, had an amazing ability to find the best markets to buy into.

For the most part, she persuaded her mother to buy and hold and not to sell, except occasionally. When the market tanked, like in October 1987, the Friday before the crash, she told her mother to move her stocks into bonds. Her broker said she was crazy because this was the middle of one of the strongest Bull Markets ever seen. But he moved her stocks into bonds anyway, telling her she was being foolish.

By Tuesday, the day after Black Monday, when the market went down over 40%, her bonds shot up over 200%, as investors looked for a safe place for their money. Charlie then went right back into stocks and swooped up incredible bargains, making millions of dollars in less than a week. Her broker quit his job the next day and went on a mission with his church to the African Congo. That turned out to be a much safer haven for him than being a stock broker.

Her mother joked to Zenadia, "What do you call a stock broker after Black Monday?" Zenadia shrugged. "A waiter!" her mother said with a grin. They both laughed hysterically. It was one of the few times Zenadia, was truly happy, but then the darkness would set in, and she had to deal with it.

Inside, she harbored a desire to right all of those who had wronged her mother over the years, starting with Bill Treese. Inwardly, she knew that her mother and Bill had been lovers and had been close. She knew she was part of the reason they were not together, but as adults, they had chosen their own paths.

He went to the Amazon, the place of her birth, and her mother took her back to the United States. They could have gotten back together, but her mother's shame at the way the rescue mission had turned out, and the way her superiors had treated her, kept her away from him permanently.

It was only as she entered her early teen years that Zenadia started to fully understand her mother, what she was and what she had been. But it didn't matter. She was devoted to her, and would see that justice was served. It was Zenadia's ability to move and affect nature around her that made her more and more aware that she had powers others did not. And she began to use those powers.

She persuaded her mother to take her to Haiti, supposedly

to go on a mission trip to help refugees. As part of investing their wealth, her mother had set up several charities, some as tax write-offs, but others, such as those that helped orphaned children, like the one in Haiti, were near and dear to Charlie's heart.

So, they went to Haiti for two weeks, sometimes into the nicer ports, other times into the bowels of hellish slums and jungles. They were treated like royals, and so, when some of the older women, asked if they could take Zenadia to play with their children, Charlie thought it would be okay. After all, she had never played with children back in the States.

But they were actually taking Zenadia to educate her. The women of Haiti knew she had the way about her and she was, obviously, a girl of power, despite her tender years.

They taught her about witchcraft, voodoo, hexes, curses and spells. Zenadia knew all of this intuitively, but needed a teacher, or teachers, to show her the true demonic methods. For her part, she learned quickly and, by the time she was returned to her mother, was fully on her way to the dark side.

She spent the next several years honing her craft, clandestinely, of course. Never revealing her true powers, even to her mother. She kept that hidden inside.

Zenadia also learned to hate. Again, from watching carefully all of those who came into contact with her mother, the good and the bad. Her mother was the only person she could never hurt or hate. But anyone else, whom she felt had hurt or slighted her mother, would be dealt with accordingly, although quietly, in what often looked like an unfortunate accident.

Her powers began to grow upon herself, until she would eventually be fully consumed by them. Once, her mother insisted they go to a funeral service for a dear friend of hers, who had helped them both over the years in many ways. The service was to be held in a beautiful Catholic Church in Walnut Creek, just down the road. Zenadia, now in her early twenties, refused politely, saying funerals made her upset for days afterwards. Her mother, thinking she had never been to a funeral service in her life, insisted. Zenadia, shrugged and agreed to go along.

When they got to the church, Zenadia, said she would stay in the car until her mother and everyone else went inside. Then she would come in, stand at the back, watch the service and then go back to the car before the others came out. That was her compromise. Her mother nodded her head and agreed.

She looked at her daughter. Zenadia's eyes burned as she looked away from her. Her mother, feeling uneasy, left the car and walked hastily to the church.

Zenadia waited until it looked as if everyone had entered the church. Then she he got out of the car and walked slowly to the building. In the entryway, she looked up at the Divinity on the Cross, hanging over the altar. The church was packed with people. She could see the open casket in the front of the pulpit.

She stood next to the cup of holy water, for the offering. It was in a large entryway, separated from the main pulpit and pews by a hallway, so that it was mostly hidden from the congregation, unless they turned around and looked, which would be disrespectful to the service. She smiled, and as she brought her hand over the holy water, it began to froth and churn.

"Rightly so," she thought and knew if she touched it, terrible things would happen then and there. So, she wisely pulled her hand back and smiled toward the body of the woman who had

been their friend. Anything more would have been blasphemous. She turned and walked out, long before the service even began.

Years later, she heard about her enemy Bill Treese's escapades in the jungles and on the Amazon, sometimes from her mother and sometimes on her own, because by now, she was able to move and see freely around the world. It was as though walls, distance and time didn't matter to her anymore.

It was about then that she was able to start communicating with animals and nature. She began to be able to bend them to her will to do what she asked of them. Unlike her enemies, she treated nature with respect.

Bill and the people he was close to were always on Zenadia's radar. There were many other people she had issues with, but Bill, the one who let her fall out of the helicopter and the one who let her mother take the blame for the debacle in Viet Nam, was the final prize to avenger her and her mother.

When she heard that the man, Reichen, whom they thought would be likely to defeat Treese the last time and, who was distantly connected to her mother and her friend the Financier, named Andres, (whom she loathed almost as much as Bill), would soon be coming to them to ask for help, she was happy. Her long-dreamed-of plan would soon be realized.

She had waited in the shadows while her mother talked to Thomas Reichen and then to the Financier. She came out of the shadows after Reichen had left. She felt the Financier run his fat, lizard-like eyes over her young body and felt his lust for her. It lubricated her sexually, not because of his lust and what he might do with her, given the chance, but knowing what she would do with him and that his ultimate fate would be at her mercy.

She left the living room and went to her room. She pressed an unseen button over the fireplace, causing the hidden door on the wall next to the bookcase, to slide back, revealing a narrow passage leading back into a corridor. As she entered, the wall slid back into place silently. Low lights came on and she walked back several feet, passing three doors on her right and then, entering a larger door at the end of the hall on her left.

These were her private chambers. Complete with a Pentagram on the floor, an altar, human skulls, animal skeletons and large tapestries depicting many hedonistic, evil scenes out of ancient times. Candles burned, incense smoldered, and the heavy atmosphere was pervasive. Standing in front of the altar, she shrugged off her clothes and stood naked in front of the burning candles. A tall mirror reflected her lean, dark, muscular body. She was trembling slightly, her large breasts heaving, she thought about the Financier. She could see him. She wanted him to see what he would never possess.

Andres was talking to her mother as they were standing in front of the large window looking out at Mt. Diablo. He had finished his brandy and was heading back to the circular bar for a refill. For some reason, he stopped and looked at the large mahogany-framed, glass floor mirror next to the sofa. It stood over eight feet tall, and was propped up by an enormous steel rod, which was anchored into the floor. It stood by itself, away from the wall. He stared at his reflection. As he started to turn away, Zenadia blinked and her image suddenly appeared - sharp, fully nude - as if she were standing right in front of him.

He gasped and stared at her for several seconds. His empty brandy snifter, fell out of his hands and landed on the thick carpet, rolling away. She smiled at him, licking her lips seductively. He felt a bulge growing in his groin and smiled back at her as his eyes roamed over her body.

The mirror's glass and the frame began to dissolve. As if in a dream, she moved toward him. Her body was only inches from him; he could smell her, a wild, intoxicating scent out of the jungle. He stared at her. He reached out and began to caress her breasts, soft, full and warm, pinching her large nipples between his thumb and fingers. He bent over to suck her left nipple, and she let him.

With her right hand, she reached down and, caressing his groin, undid his pants, allowing them to fall to the floor. Slowly bending down, she reached under his underpants and caressed his stiffening member, beneath the fat folds of his belly.

She pulled away from his mouth and, bending over, used her mouth to minister to him orally. Still stroking her breasts, he began to moan, wondering what Charlie behind him was thinking. Suddenly, as the wave started rising over him, he began to orgasm into her sweet mouth, but just as suddenly, she was gone - and he was facing the mirror, with his pants on the ground, and him discharging all over the glass. In horror, he looked behind him, with Charlie, her back to the window, staring at him, with her arms folded. He grabbed his pants and ran for the bathroom. Charlie smiled and turned back to the window.

In her room, Zenadia spat out the man's semen into a skull head cup made from a real skull bone, sitting on the altar. She had his seed now, and he would pay. Beside herself with lust and excitement, she fell to the floor and masturbated frantically.

CHAPTER FIVE

CLOSING IN ON THE VILLAGE

BILL TREESE HAD BEEN AT THE HELM of the PT boat all day. After the attempt on their lives by the two fighter planes, he had become wary of what might be up the river. Never one to be overly fearful, Bill was, nonetheless, a cautious man. You had to be cautious to survive on this part of the river, and in this jungle.

Now, of course, the enemy had shown their hand. Those planes did not come from enemy Chibcha Indians, or any other tribe, for that matter. The prize on his head or the heads of his crew had to be pretty high, for someone to risk an open attack on an armed vessel, especially a PT boat.

Deep in thought, he wondered who could be behind the attack. They had to be well-financed, well-connected and well-organized. Their intelligence also had to be very good, or how else could they have found him so precisely, this deep in the jungle, and on this river?

It was nearing suppertime, and, right on cue, Manolo appeared on deck. He was sad about his friend Julian, who had been killed this morning. Bill was sad too, and the others had been stunned into silence. They had gone back and found his body floating in the river. Bill had wrapped his body up in a heavy sheet and placed him on the stern deck. Then they went to a village upriver from the battle, where Bill was friendly with the Chief. The Chief knew of Julian, and said they would get him back to his family. That was the best Bill could hope for.

"*Capitán* Bill," said Manolo, "Let me take over, so you can eat and rest some before the night hits us."

Bill smiled. He was actually really hungry, because he hadn't eaten all day. Too much to do, and no appetite. *But*, he thought, *survival first.*

"Did you eat, yet, Manolo? Bill inquired.

"*Si.*"

"Ok, then," Bill heaved himself up from the standing deck chair and went below.

In the galley, he found Jack, and Kimmi toying with their food.

Bill cleared his throat. "Hi, guys. I guess no one is very hungry." He looked at the steaming pot of native greens, the pile of beans and rice, and on the counter, the whole fish that Monolo had prepared. Sighing, Bill helped himself to a good portion of each dish. He sat down at the small table and started eating.

"First order of business, nourishment. It will keep you alive and I don't have to remind you about what happened the last time we went up in these waters." He paused. "Or what happened this morning," he added.

"So, dig in. That's an order!" he smiled.

Kimmi looked up and smiled back. "Ok." Jack nodded his

head and started to eat again.

Bill stood up and reached into one of the food lockers behind him. He took out a bottle of local rum and three glasses.

"Here, have a jar of this," he said while pouring out a stiff shot for them. "It will help to calm your nerves and help you sleep some in a couple of hours."

They both took their glasses and drank gratefully.

"Did Julian have family?" Kimmi asked.

"No parents. Both passed. A few cousins, and maybe a brother or two he didn't keep in touch with. He will still be missed by his village, but no mom or dad anguishing over him.

"Everyone on this river knows life can be cheap, and can end suddenly. It is sad, but it is reality. It's OK to feel bad for him, but don't dwell on it. Keep focused on our mission at hand. It will likely get worse before it gets better."

"Who sent those planes to attack us?" asked Jack. "That was no random attack by a local pilot's organization reliving the glory days of World War Two. Those guys were out to stop us permanently, not capture us!"

Bill rubbed his chin thoughtfully. "You're right, Doc. You hit the nail on the head. They had to be well-financed and had strong motivation. Also, good intel, because no one knows we're up here."

"What about Thomas Reichen? He escaped and he is probably trying to get back to the Lost City to get his hands on the gold again."

Kimmi added, "This time he knows what he's up against and he won't be stopped."

"I thought of that," Bill agreed. "I know he has resources, but he doesn't have the money or the brains to pull that kind of an attack off. But you are right about one thing. He is well-motivated and will do everything he can not to be stopped. He's a smart cookie; we can't underestimate him. But I think there is another player, or players, behind this whole thing."

"The government?" asked Jack.

"No. They're too lazy and too vulnerable. They know they don't have to do anything, and will still get a share of the gold. So why risk it?"

They were quiet as they went back to their food and thought about what Bill had said.

Kimmi asked, "When you were transporting him down the Amazon to prison, did he say anything to you about his contacts in the U.S. or around the world?"

Bill smiled. "No, he didn't show me his little black book, if that's what you mean."

They both smiled back.

"I did ask him once if he had served in the U.S. Service or in Special Forces. I told him I was impressed and, since we had a long way to go on the trip, would he like to share some war stories. He declined, of course, but I did ask him if he was in-country, or, in other words, did he serve in Viet Nam. He did say yes, but that was all he would volunteer."

"Can't say I blame him," said Jack.

"The way he fought me on the deck of my boat, and the way he fought with the natives, told me he had to have some Special Forces training from the D.O.D."

"D.O.D?" asked Kimmi.

"Department of Defense. Probably a Marine, or a Navy

S.E.A.L. Maybe even an Army Ranger or C.I.A. Who knows?" he shrugged.

Both Kimmi and Jack were starting to yawn, which made Bill yawn also.

"You two go get some sleep. I'm going to check with Manolo and, if he's ok, grab a few zzzz's myself. Manolo and I will take the watch tonight. Tomorrow, you can both lend a hand. We're supposed to pick up a medical doctor in the next town on the river to take him to the village, to treat Cornelia's son Damien, who is lying sick. The doctor is an expert in exotic diseases, and they think he can help Damien."

"What about my dad?" asked Kimmi angrily. "We have to get to him!"

"We will. John is your dad, but he is also my dear friend, and Jack's too. We won't be delayed. The natives are doing their best to get to him. We're fighting on two fronts." He looked up toward the low ceiling, as though it were the sky. "Maybe more than two fronts," he said.

Jack and Kimmi nodded and got up to go to their bunks, while Bill went up the ladder to check on Manolo.

Dawn came early, as it always seemed to happen on the Amazon. Night was dark and silent. The monkeys screamed almost all night until about 3 A.M, when mercifully, they stopped, for whatever reason. Then there was an unearthly silence, sometimes disturbed by the deep growl of a predator, but mostly silence until dawn.

The atmosphere was thick and often seemed evil, especially if you were not accustomed to it, meaning from birth. The Indians did not fear the jungle, but they also did not venture out into it at night. Nighttime was when the predators fed and that's why, more than anything, there was silence.

Then there was the river. Always the river. The mighty Amazon flowed through an entire continent, through three countries, starting humbly as a mere spring in the Peruvian Andes, it flows east and exits as a mass of millions of cubic feet of fresh water into the Atlantic Ocean - over 4,000 miles from its source. The jungle was green, but the river was brown. Murky, dark, sometimes sinister, it had a life of its own. It was never predictable. Often tame, it could whip up in an instant and cause damage locally, and also hundreds of miles downriver.

The floods would wipe out thousands of acres of shoreline, causing mass uprooting of trees, brush and plants. Everything wound up into the river, and was usually dumped many miles downstream. Rolling logs were often a cause for alarm for the many sailors of the Amazon. Unseen, floating just below the surface, they could rip the bow out of the steamers, boats and ships that moved up and down the mighty river, causing them to sink quickly with a loss of life and cargo.

Bill Treese held his binoculars tightly to his eyes, searching the distant bend of the river. It was 7:30 A.M., and the light was gaining momentum over the thick trees in the jungle on either side of the river. He was close to the village where he had to pick up the doctor he would take to the Chibchas, to help the young Prince Damien.

Everyone else was asleep. Manolo had spelled him at the helm until 0500, and then Bill, who had snapped awake without an alarm, relieved him on-deck. Bill had quickly knocked back two cups of coffee and brought a third cup on-deck. The coffee had been started earlier by Manolo, who had lashed down the wheel, reduced the ship's speed, then ran below-deck, started the pot and then raced back up topside.

This was all preplanned and was actually a routine of theirs. Bill never slept much. Just enough to keep him sharp, and he knew, as he got older, there would be less sleep in store for him. He sighed, lowering his binoculars. It was a curse, this so-called "freedom of self-employment" on the river. Work for yourself and be free! He chuckled at the irony.

It was still cool in the early morning hours. Almost enough to make him shiver, but not quite. It would take them three more hours to get to the village, assuming the doctor was ready to go. Another player he had to protect. He shook his head. He should put in for overtime, but he was not even being paid for this trip. It was just to save John and the baby. He sat down heavily on the standing deck chair and took a long sip of the hot coffee. Oh, well, he shrugged.

Suddenly the hairs on the back of his neck stood up on their own. Bill immediately felt that something bad was waiting for them up the river. He shook his head, but could not shake the strong feeling. He grabbed the binoculars, and searched the water upriver.

At first, he saw nothing. Then, off in the distance, he saw something that made his blood run cold.

Approximately 10,000 yards upstream, Bill could see a periscope ripping through the water, heading straight for them!

Bill flipped a switch on the console. General Quarters rang out, alerting the others, who were sleeping below, that there was another emergency situation on deck.

Bill increased speed. He was ready to attack, and the fact there was a periscope up ahead indicated to him it was not friendly. Especially considering the attack from the two warplanes yesterday.

Jack, Kimmiko and Manolo shot up on deck through the bulkhead to the deck, shaking and frightened. Jack spoke first, "What the hell now?" he asked.

Bill motioned up ahead. "There is a periscope, and I doubt he's friendly. Jack, get on the starboard gun. Kimmi, get on the port gun. Manolo, get on the aft Oerlikon gun. We may need it. Everybody put on helmets and life jackets just in case. Now move!"

Everyone jumped to their positions and reported in when they were ready.

Bill increased his speed. He knew the imminent danger of the machine guns on the deck of the submarine, but the real danger came from the torpedoes. At the moment the submarine was submerged, probably 10 feet under the surface. He couldn't tell how big it was, but knew it was probably a small-to-medium sub. Certainly not a large one because it would be too big for the river. In any event, it appeared to be hostile. Suddenly, two water plumes jettisoned upward as the submarine's launch mechanisms fired off two torpedoes heading straight at the PT boat.

Bill could see the torpedoes heading for them. "Fish in the water!" he screamed, and thrust his throttle forward, running into the path of the two torpedoes.

Jack screamed above the roar of the engines, "What the hell are you doing?!"

Bill, with his face set into a grimace, pushed the throttle forward, picking up even more speed.

Kimmi popped up in the port gun turret, hanging onto the twin machine gun firing handle for dear life, and looked forward in alarm. Manolo appeared next to Captain Bill, who had a wild look on his face. For all of Manolo, Captain Bill looked like the devil himself.

Suddenly the two torpedoes appeared near the surface in the water, heading straight for them.

Bill, heading into the attack, did not waver. In fact, he seemed content to force himself directly into their path.

Bill lowered his head. Looking forward, he smiled in anticipation.

Five seconds later, the first torpedo bounced off the hull of the PT Boat harmlessly.

Bill juked the boat to the right, and the second torpedo passed by.

"What the hell? " said Jack in astonishment.

Bill looked over from the console. "Combat maneuver, Jack. It didn't have time to arm itself."

"What about the other one?!" Jack screamed above the roar of the engines.

"That one is looking for us now," Bill said ruefully.

Suddenly, Bill's boat was almost over the submerged submarine and he began to talk to himself, as if going down a checklist.

"Set depth charges. Ten feet." He spun a dial on the console. The crew heard two loud clicks on two of the aft depth charges. "Aggressor Number 1, Number 2, count now! 5 4 3 2 1, set aggressor path and execute! Path executed!" he yelled.

He pressed two adjoining buttons on the console simultaneously. Two depth charges, one on the port side and one on the starboard side, rolled off the stern deck with a burst of steam, as the PT boat shot by its intended target, almost running over the periscope, which had been coming straight at them. Bill increased his speed to the maximum. He didn't bother to look back, knowing that the submarine was already starting its turnaround to follow him.

Suddenly there was a tremendous explosion, as the depth charges hit their mark! The submarine launched halfway out of the water and then split in two. Jack, Kimmi and Manolo turned back to see the two halves of the sub rise out of the water, with an explosive roar! They landed right back onto the surface, and then sank immediately. Pieces of metal rained down, but the PT boat was already two hundred yards ahead of the wreckage, and going for more.

As they shot up the river, more metal fragments rained down all around them.

Bill yelled, "Look for the fish! Look for the fish!"

At first, they thought about the giant piranha, but then they realized the Captain was talking about the torpedo. Kimmi and Jack spun around in their gun turrets looking behind them and also to the sides of the boat. Manolo ran back to the Oerlikon gun and looked back. He could see a ripple in the water from behind that was coming straight at them. It was gaining speed and catching up to them.

He screamed at Bill, "*Capitán* Bill, it is back there!"

Bill looked back. He turned to look ahead, then snapped on the radar screen, where he could see the blip following them. After making a fast calculation in his head, he began to look for the shore; he had made a quick decision.

"Everyone strap yourselves in!" he screamed. "If we go under, make sure you can unhitch yourself, or you will go to the bottom with her!"

Jack shouted back, "What if it hits us?"

"Then it won't matter!" yelled Bill.

Jack, Kimmi and Manolo all snapped on their harnesses, which were fixed to their machine guns. Jack shoved his helmet down hard on his head and then checked his life jacket. Kimmi and Manolo all did the same thing.

Bill was looking intently at the radar screen. The blip was practically on top of them. He increased his speed. Downriver, he saw what he was looking for; a sharp bend to the right. Fortunately, it was a wide spot, because there wasn't much room to maneuver. He immediately shoved the throttle all the way forward.

Jack could see the approaching bend in the river getting closer. They were going over 50 miles per hour, but it felt like a lot more because of the openness of the boat. He suddenly realized Bill was heading straight into the shore!

"What are you doing?!" he screamed at Bill.

But Bill never acknowledged him, and just kept staring at the radar screen. He looked up at the bend in the river, which was getting closer. Just to make sure, he glanced back where he could verify the torpedo's position was in the water. It was heading directly for his stern!

Kimmi, looking straight ahead, no longer thinking of the torpedo, which was almost about to hit them, was thinking about how she could jump off this damn boat, but that would likely kill her instantly.

Manolo took his eyes off the torpedo for a moment and looked forward. He could see the rocky shore directly in front of them, with the jungle trees towering overhead. He started to panic and, in addition to his harness, threw his arms around his gun and dropped to his knees.

Only Bill remained calm. He began counting under his breath. The roar of the engines, the approaching shore, and the torpedo almost on top of him, were all lost to him as he went deep inside his mind.

"Sounding collision," he said quietly, while pulling a lever on the console to his right. A loud siren started wailing, even louder than the "Battle Stations" horn.

"We're going to die!" Jack shouted, as they were almost on top of the shore.

Kimmi began screaming.

Suddenly, Bill spun his wheel hard to the right, as he cut the power to his starboard engine. The effect heeled the heavy boat over on its right side, almost submerging Jack in its violent yaw. Had Kimmi not been strapped in, she would have flown over Bill's head and into the water. Manolo hit his head against the cannon and was thrown violently over onto his back, with only the safety strap saving him from being ejected also.

The torpedo, still going forward, slammed into the rocky shore and blew up with a tremendous explosion!

For the second time, debris rained down on the escaping PT boat. Rocks, dirt, river water and huge parts of trees fell on and around it.

Bill had already straightened the wheel and reignited the starboard engine, so they would not keep circling to the right. The boat shot forward heading down the river at breakneck speed.

Jack was the first to recover, "You almost killed us! I don't know who is worse, the enemy or you! What the hell are you doing?" he yelled angrily at Bill. "We need to stop this right now!"

Bill didn't say anything. He began to slow the boat down, before the engines overheated, blew up or shut down completely. He glanced over at Kimmi, only to barely see the top of her hair as she cowered down in the port gun turret and then he looked back at Manolo who was slumped over the gun, alive but possibly hurt.

He glanced over at Jack, who was blazing with anger and, if the truth be known, mostly with fear.

Bill turned to face Jack as he continued to throttle down the boat.

"I wasn't trying to kill US," he said as he emphasized the "us," "but I tried and did save ALL of US! Twice, in fact, in the past 24 hours! There is no stopping now. There is no going back. There are probably more people trying to stop us and maybe kill us, but we will deal with that as it comes up."

His voice started to rise. "John needs us. The baby needs us. Just like the last time, it is either kill or be killed. So, you need to grab yourself a big set of nuts and get on board with this mission!"

Kimmi, rising up in the gun turret, said meekly, "What should I grab, Uncle Bill?" She smiled and that helped to break the tension.

Bill smiled, shook his head and looked toward the heavens. "I'm getting too old for this."

Jack and Kimmi both climbed out of the turrets.

"Can you two check on Manolo, please?"

They both ran back to where he was slumped against the cannon.

"You OK?" Kimmi asked.

"*Si*," came the weak reply. "I'm OK. Hit my head on the gun when we turned, but my head is clearing now."

"He OK?" yelled Bill.

"Yeah," Jack said. He looked over at Kimmi, who was looking at Manolo with concern. She still had strong feelings for him.

"Let's take him below, so I can examine his head. Then I'll make us some breakfast, so our cook can rest a little."

Jack and Kimmi made their way to the bridge holding Manolo between them.

"I'll make us some breakfast," Jack said to Bill. He was still mad, but realized Bill was right. Plus, he was the Captain, and Jack didn't want to walk the plank!

"Can you make us a hot breakfast?" Bill said hopefully. He was wet, and starting to shiver a little.

Jack glanced back at him as they started to take Manolo down below.

"Sure. Peanut butter on toast!" He smiled as Bill grimaced. He continued to scan the instruments on his console to make sure the engines were ok. Then he started to rev up the boat's engines for the trip to the village to pick up the medical doctor.

Surprisingly, to everyone except Jack, the breakfast he whipped up on short notice was amazing. Down below, Kimmi got Manolo into his bunk while applying an ice pack onto his forehead, which was now bruising up nicely. She asked Jack if he needed help, but he told her to stay with Manolo. He had already given Manolo a full medical checkup and determined he did not have a concussion, just a headache. He told Kimmi to tell him if Manolo felt dizzy or nauseous, both bad signs. Manolo was feeling better every minute, but Kimmi would not let him out of bed and stayed by his side, tending to him. They held hands like before, and whispered fondly to each other.

Jack, after surveying Manolo's well-ordered galley, began to make scrambled eggs with cheese and onions mixed in, along with a special blend of spices. He also made bacon, hash browns, toast and pancakes. He brought one full plate to Kimmi and Manolo, with instructions to eat slowly and drink water. He thought it best that they share, but let them know there was more on the stove. Kimmi giggled as she fed Manolo like a baby, teasing him with pieces of toast.

Next, Jack made a big plate for Bill and a smaller one for himself. He brought them up to the bridge, where Bill was driving the boat at a moderate speed. The heat of the late morning had dried him off, and he was feeling better.

"Here ya go, Captain," Jack said, officially handing Bill the larger plate. He reached into his back pocket and pulled out two small bottles of orange juice.

"Wow. Thanks Jack. This looks great! I love Manolo's cooking, but it seems like everything he makes has some hot green peppers in it."

They both laughed.

"Say, Bill. Sorry about me shooting my mouth off back there. It was stupid, but I was really scared. It won't happen again," his voice trailed off.

Bill smiled at him. "I've already forgotten about it. I respect a man who says what's on his mind, even when he's wrong!" They both laughed.

Bill looked down at his plate, which was suddenly empty. He

wiped off his mouth on his sleeve and looked away with a little guilt.

"Want some more?" Jack asked with a smile.

Bill nodded his head. "Maybe just some of the eggs."

Jack nodded, set his plate down and started to go below.

"Hey, Jack. Uh, maybe a couple of pieces more of bacon and a short stack of pancakes too, please."

Jack laughed and said okay. He returned a few minutes later with a full plate and smiled as he handed it to Bill.

"Thanks, Jack. You cook even better than you shoot!"

"I'll take that as a compliment!" They both laughed.

"How's Manolo?"

"He'll be OK. He'll have a headache for a couple of days, but nothing serious. No concussion, that I can tell."

"OK. Thanks. You're a great doc."

"OK. How much longer until we get there?"

"About two more hours, to refuel at the village and to pick up the doctor. Then it will take us 18 hours to get to the Lost El Dorado, assuming we don't meet up with more bad guys."

Jack grabbed both plates. "Ok, I'll go clean up and then if you can show me how to drive this tub, you can go below and clean up a bit too."

"That sounds like a plan. Thanks, Jack!"

Two hours later, they were pulling up to the village dock, which was more like a floating pier. Several Natives jumped on the boat as it slowly pulled in and helped to secure her.

Jack stayed on the deck, discreetly standing next to Bill's Winchester rifle, which was kept out of sight. Manolo and Kimmi stayed below deck, while two large Natives escorted Bill to the

Chief's hut. The Chief and Bill embraced, but there was no time to talk, as they had to hurry.

Bill was then told the shocking news that the doctor had gone on ahead, already summoned by the Chibcha tribe, who were desperate to get him to the village to treat the child, Prince Damien. Several of the Natives had shown up in a small boat with a fast engine to transport him there. They didn't know how the Natives had obtained the boat, but it was probably through the gold and their contacts with the outside world.

Bill shrugged and asked how much fuel they had to sell to him. He was told a few hundred gallons. He actually needed more than that, but was glad to take what he could get. Once the fuel was loaded onto the boat, and the Chief was paid with a combination of cash and cases of beer, Bill took over the helm and they were on their way.

Bill was looking at getting no sleep that night, but a couple of hours later, Manolo made his way to the bridge and said he felt good enough to drive the boat until at least until dark, which was about five hours away.

Jack had made dinner, just hamburgers and potato chips, but they were good and were quickly devoured by all. Bill went to sleep, and Jack and Kimmi went up on deck to keep Manolo company.,

Once it was dark, Bill rejoined them. While driving the boat, he explained what they would be doing. Their main mission was to find John and get him out of the cave. Since the doctor had gone on ahead to treat the baby, this simplified things.

Bill told them to all go below and get as much sleep as they could muster. It had been a long day, and they needed to rest. The next few days were going to be extremely busy and they had to focus. They were all sure that whoever had tried to stop them, had a motive and probably would not give up easily. Their lives were at stake.

CHAPTER SIX

FLIGHT TO THE JUNGLE

THE ONLY TIME ZENADIA WAS vulnerable involved the moments before she woke up. Before that, from the time of sleep to the time of wakefulness, she could see in her inner eye what was around her. Because of what and who she was, her survival depended on it.

But for four or five minutes before waking up, she dropped into a deep, coma-like sleep, during which she went completely blank.

Charlie, her mother, knew this from the time Zenadia was a baby. She would never hurt her daughter, but she knew she still had to be able to control her. Like a wild animal in captivity, Zenadia was there because she knew she was safer here than in the wilds, and so she would be vulnerable to the only person she trusted in the world. Her mother never betrayed that trust.

So, in that moment, Charlie went to Zenadia's bed and, timing herself, gently shook her daughter awake.

Zenadia's eyes snapped awake in an instant. "Is it time?" she asked.

Charlie nodded.

Zenadia threw back the covers. The room was still dark, but Charlie knew her daughter slept in only a loincloth and so she looked away.

"I'll be waiting for you."

Zenadia acted like she didn't hear her as she threw her clothes on, grabbed a pre-packed bag and a backpack loaded with the things she would need.

She went straight to the garage, where the 1937 Rolls Royce Phantom III, driven by the servant Jones, was waiting for her. She joined Charlie in the back seat, after tossing her gear into the trunk.

She turned to Charlie, who was wearing flight fatigues. "What about Reichen?"

"He's not flying with us. He will meet us in Bogota, and then a chopper will take us from there."

Charlie glanced up at Jones, who could not hear them through the glass. She pressed a button on her seat. "Take us to Buchanan Field, Jones. Please," she added. She never told anyone about their planned journeys, whether they were for two hours or two days. Clandestine military training had taught her that. "After you drop us off, I will call you to pick us up."

Jones nodded silently, knowing it could be at any hour of the day or night - just like this morning, when he was summoned at 3:30 A. M. by Charlie to have the car ready in an hour, maybe two.

The ride to Concord was quick. It was 5:25 A. M., so the

commute traffic along Highway 680 had not yet started.

They pulled up to the East Ramp at Buchanan Field Airport in Concord, and got out of the car. Charlie and Zenadia walked up to the Cessna Citation X, which was warmed up and waiting for them. With a stock top speed of Mach 0.935, it was the fastest small private jet in the world. However, this one had been modified to go over Mach 1, the speed of sound. Charlie had not reached that speed in many years, and only then, in an Air Force jet. But, just in case, her flight suit was pressurized, so she would not black out at high speeds or when pulling G's. This was an added safety measure, as the cabin and the cockpit of the Cessna were also pressurized.

Charlie went up to the tall, dark man standing at the ladder leading to the cockpit.

"Everything checked, Ackers?"

"*Ya*," he said in a thick German accent. "*Zie ist gut!*"

Charlie narrowed her eyes. "And the fuel tanks? Topped off?"

"*Ya!*"

Charlie stepped into the cockpit and began preparations to take off. She made all of her pre-flight checks and flipped on the switches to start the plane. She still checked the fuel levels on her own, and affirmed that they were full. The people who worked for her had been with her for over a decade, and were well-paid. There was no incentive for them to not do their job well. Zenadia had settled into the front passenger seat and picked up her iPad.

"Close the hatch. Prepare to get underway." Charlie contacted Ground Control and made her way to Runway 32 Right, the largest at the field.

Charlie pushed the throttle forward and taxied out to the

warm-up area. There she ran the plane through its second pre-flight preparations. She then taxied to the runway apron.

"Tower, 787 Foxtrot Niner Niner, in position for takeoff."

"Roger, 787 Foxtrot Niner Niner, you are cleared for takeoff."

With that, she pushed the throttle forward and with a jump, the plane took off into the early morning dawn.

****

Andres Rameriez was not only rich, he was an industrialist, a computer programmer and also, an international slave trader. He was the money behind the selling of women and young girls from all over the world. He arranged kidnapping, drug abuse and the imprisonment of young women to become sex slaves to his many clients. He fancied himself to be an international playboy, but was none of that. In reality, he was just a pimp.

He had no feelings about those whose lives he put in danger. He had learned that lesson well from his father and mother, who had slaves and imprisoned hundreds of girls from all over South America.

He was interested in very young girls, the younger the better, to whet his appetites.

Driving away from Charlie's estate in his own limousine, he thought about her slutty daughter Zenadia.

He had no idea what had happened. It was like a dream. She had suddenly appeared right in front of him completely nude. He smelled her. He felt her. He tasted her and then, while he orgasmed, she disappeared. He was facing his own reflection while he shot his load onto the huge mirror in front of Charlie, with his pants down around his ankles.

He ran to the bathroom, cleaned up and called his limousine to pick him up immediately, which they did. He did not return to the living room to face Charlie.

He made his way to the airport and settled aboard his Lear Jet. The pilot took off as soon as possible. He was stopping first in Houston, Texas, where he was going to pick up a fresh girl for a few hours, before flying home to Dallas to make preparations. In two days, he would be flying to South America. While still taxiing to the runway, Andres, got out of his seat, grabbed a large glass from the on-board bar and filled it with ice, scotch and soda water. Then he slammed it down at the bar, and then refilled his glass. He then sat back down in his seat with a full glass, but had easy access to more drinks whenever he wanted one.

Andres was angry. Besides the money to be made, which there was a lot, he had scores to settle.

He was ready to settle all accounts, but he was also ready to kill a lot of people, if need be.

The more he drank, the less rational he became. He was going to kill both Charlie and Zenadia, once the job was done. He would kill the Chibcha Indians and keep their village. He would sell most of the gold on the open market and the clandestine gold on the black market. Either way, he would make a fortune! Then there was the cocaine to consider. There were umpteen billions of dollars to make with the cocaine cash crop that was there, which had not yet been touched.

He sat back in the front seat of the jet and put his hands behind his head. His own band of American mercenaries would be waiting for him at the military airport near Bogota. He had

Native mercenaries there too, so they would have no problems moving into place among the locals to intercept the Americans.

He drank some more and thought about Zenadia. Maybe he would only kill Charlie and keep the girl for himself, or sell her on the open market to the highest bidder, if she would not behave. He fantasized tying her down and spending hours using her young body for his pleasure. He began to get aroused again, so he stared out the window, trying to get himself under control. He smiled when he thought about the girl in Texas waiting for him, a sixteen-year-old runaway. The plane was almost at altitude, so he got up and poured another scotch, then sat down and leaned back in his seat.

Life was good.

****

Charlie's plane ripped down through the cloud-covered skies of the late afternoon and landed on the tarmac of the Bogota Airport, which, as it happened, was also named the El Dorado Airport. She had made arrangements to land here with the help of the tower, because this was controlled airspace. She was directed to Runway 13R, with its wide-open approach. But when they landed, instead of being handed over to ground control to be led to a certain taxiway, they were released by ground, to traverse on their own to Ramp X. That one was used for clandestine drug drops and so was given a wide berth by the authorities. As she taxied in, a green jeep with a machine gun mount escorted her to her slip. She made preparations to stop; the engines were shut off and slowly wound down.

Out of her window, she saw that several other jeeps had joined the first one. There was no alarm; she would be joined by local mercenaries who were here to help her. They had been paid half their fee in advance and were promised 25% more when they made contact with the village, and the rest when they finished the job with the village and the Natives. Whether the Chibchas were taken alive or wanted to fight to the death was up to them.

She secured the aircraft, peeled off her flight suit down to her jungle fatigues and went to the back of the plane to get her daughter.

Zenadia, was staring out the window at the soldiers and the jeeps. "Who are they?" she asked Charlie.

"Our escorts. They are taking us as to the jungle, where there are helicopters waiting. Then we will fly near the City of the El Dorado. We will land and attack the village."

"What about Bill Treese?"

"He was spotted on the Amazon with the doctor and the daughter of the Professor. The Financier, Andres, sent two fighter planes and a small submarine to stop him and keep him out of the village, but they were not successful. I told him he needed to plant men with stinger missiles on the shore and then hit them when they weren't looking. But he wanted to do it his way. He is too macho to just take them out. He had to make a big show with his military might, which failed,"- Charlie rolled her eyes upward.

"I told him that Treese, for whatever we think about him would be a formidable opponent, and a hard man to take down." She shook her head.

She continued, "Now it will be more difficult to take the village if Treese is there. He will likely be tied up trying to get his friend out of the collapsed cave, if he is not already dead. "

"Wait, the doctor they sent to help the baby out is on board his boat?" Zenadia asked.

"No, I think this is a different doctor from our area. The one they are bringing in to help the baby is from down here. I don't know if he is onboard or not."

Zenadia smiled. "No doctor on earth will be able to save that child. Once he is dead, the village will know they are cursed, and will give up to us without a fight."

Charlie looked at her. "Will you reverse the voodoo curse once we take over the village, or will it be too late?" Charlie was uneasy about killing the baby Prince if it was not necessary. If they were found out, the parents could go insane with rage and could be a problem for them.

"I can try to time it, but there are no guarantees that he will live or die." Zenadia shrugged. "Who cares? Anyway, I want Bill Treese alive. I've waited a long time to come face-to-face with him."

Charlie nodded silently. "I understand."

They went to the bottom of the steps onto the tarmac. They were carrying two suitcases, two backpacks and two grips. One of the mercenaries who was wearing fatigues, came up to them, saluted and motioned for them to get in the back of a covered jeep. He was big, and spoke with a Colombian accent. There were sergeant's stripes on his sleeves, and he was obviously in charge.

He called for another soldier to take their bags and put them into the same jeep, but Charlie would not let go of one of the bags and shook her head at the soldier, even though she had handed over the rest of the luggage. The other jeeps drove up and surrounded their vehicle. Two in front and two in back, Military style.

As they climbed into the jeep, they were greeted by Thomas Reichen.

"Hello," he said. "Glad you made it!" Charlie sat next to him, with the bag on her lap. Zenadia sat in one of the seats opposite, and facing him. Her eyes burned into his. He blinked twice, as the smile faded from his face. He shivered in spite of himself; the girl made him nervous. Charlie had told him Zenadia would be coming, and that she could handle herself in this situation.

"So, do you have a plan?" Charlie asked, "Other than what we discussed at my house?"

"Yes. We are taking two choppers in, with the mercenaries we hired and you paid for. Do you have the money to pay them when we get to the village and also when the job is done?"

Charlie nodded and held up the bag.

"Did you bring weapons too?" he asked.

Charlie nodded again.

"OK. We are driving through the jungle to a hidden spot where we can fly the two helicopters out. The pilots are already on board. It will take us a few hours to get there. It will be dark, but the pilots know the way to get to the village. There is a spot where they will land . One helicopter will stay and one will fly back to wait for our instructions. Then we will hike in and attack the village before dawn."

Charlie looked out the window, while Zenadia continued to stare at Thomas.

"OK," Charlie said thoughtfully, "How are you going to attack them? Do you have a plan? Do you have the village mapped out, and do you know their strength? How are you planning on dealing with Bill Treese and the PT boat, with their guns onboard? Apparently, the planes and the submarine couldn't stop him. So, what are you planning to do to stop him, assuming he is not preoccupied with trying to save his friend the professor?"

Thomas smiled and looked directly at Zenadia and then back at Charlie.

"Stingers. Men on the shore with stinger missiles. How does that suit you?"

Charlie smiled, "That's what I have been saying!"

For the first time Zenadia spoke up. "I have plans for him. I want him alive, and I will deal with him myself! I don't care what you do to the kid or whoever is on the boat, but I'll take Treese myself!"

Thomas sat there looking at her. He decided to tread carefully, first because he had a bad feeling about her, and second, because he suddenly realized she could probably help them in ways he could not. Obviously, some sort of hatred for Bill Treese motivated her, but he did not know why, nor did he really care.

He smiled at her, which was difficult, because of the burning intensity that came off of her, like fire and brimstone. It was like standing too close to the sun.

"OK. We can try to figure that out when the situation arrives. We will give you priority to go after him. But please understand, the mission comes first - before personal vendettas. Having said that, the man has a tremendous ability to smell danger and get himself out of a bad situation. Not sure what you have planned for him, but I doubt he would see you as any kind of a threat. Has he ever seen you?"

Zenadia nodded and looked away, "Yes, but not since I was a baby."

"But he knows you, right, Charlie?"

"Yes."

"So, if he saw you both, would he put the two of you together?"

"Yes," she said again.

"OK. Then we'll have to figure out a way to get Zenadia close to Treese and have you be somewhere else, to carry out your part of the attack."

"What do you have in mind for me?" Charlie asked.

"I'm working on that. I do know the layout of the village, the relative strength of the Natives' numbers, and how we can hit them, probably from the back and the sides, moving them towards the river. It's rumored that the giant piranhas have started to come back, and if so, the Natives won't want to go there."

"We'll probably attack early and use some incendiary devices to set off some explosions. Take several of them when they come out of their huts, and then try to get to the baby's parents and her uncle, the Chief. If we can get them to surrender, there won't have to be a lot of bloodshed. But if we are not careful and they are prepared to repel boarders, then we will have a firefight on our hands."

Zenadia spoke up. "The giant fish are back, but not here yet. I can command them."

The hairs on the back of Thomas Reichen's neck stood up. He shivered again, not just at what she said, but because he knew that every word she said was true. He decided again to be very careful around her, and also to treat Charlie with the respect she also deserved.

"OK," he said quietly. "For some reason, I believe what you say, even though it sounds insane to me."

"Charlie, you told me in Danville that you were an expert with firearms and explosives. Did you bring anything with you? We have some light arms, some small explosives and the two stinger missiles I mentioned earlier".

"Yes," she said simply, without elaborating.

"What about your friend, the Financier? Is he coming here to help us?"

"No," said Charlie, "he's more of a silent partner. Plus, he is a coward and a dandy. He's just a pimp, but a very rich one."

Thomas reached into a small warming cabinet under his seat. He brought out three hoagie sandwiches and a large thermos of coffee. He gave them each a sandwich and poured coffee for them. "Good roast beef, on local bread, with local produce. The mustard is mixed with the area's best creamed horseradish. It's tangy, but not too hot. There are also some local kettle chips, salty and spicy, but really good."

Charlie and Thomas dug in, wiping the sauce off their mouths with large paper napkins and then drinking the hot coffee.

Zenadia placed the sandwich on the seat next to her, and drank the coffee slowly as she stared out the window at the darkening jungle passing by. She would eat later. For now, she was thinking about Bill Treese. She sent thoughts to the fish, telling them with her mind to move toward the village, then closed her eyes, forcing her will on the jungle and the elements around her.

****

Little did they know that the Financier, Andres Rameriez, was landing at a small private airport in Colombia later that day and would also be met by his own team of mercenaries, who would wait and watch from the jungle behind Thomas Reichen's party. Their job was to take away from Reichen's group whatever they were able to take away from the Chibcha Tribe.

As Andres, was moving his bulky body out of his seat and through hatch, he could see his guards lounging next to their jeeps. They were going to accompany him deep into the jungle. He wasn't sure exactly how they were going to get there, but he knew they were well-armed. He had explained how they would stay in the jungle and wait, but they also had to make sure that whatever happened in the village was over. It didn't really matter if Charlie's group won or the Chibchas won, because no one was expecting him or his group to be there to collect the spoils of the war.

He moved down the jet's stairs onto the tarmac, where he was met by his commanding officer, an American with clandestine military experience. There were about two dozen men with him, all of who looked extremely rough.

His Commanding Officer was named Caesar. He was 49 years old, about 5'10", and 175 lbs., not an ounce of fat on him. He had a Colt .45 on his side and casually slung across his back was a Browning submachine gun. He looked at Andres without humor.

"We're ready to move out."

Andres nodded, and they walked toward the helicopters that would take them to the Lost El Dorado.

****

Professor John Waales knew he had a problem. The clanking sound had stopped, but he still did not know what had caused it. While he still had light from the artificial lamps beside him, and the musty air around him, it was only a matter of time until these began to fail. He didn't even have paper to write his last notes to family and friends.

He looked upwards to where he last saw the pure gold ore - more than he could have ever have imagined. It was funny. The buildings and the altars were made of gold, but here he was, stuck in a collapsed mine, looking for more gold! Well, he had found the mother lode, only it was leaning over him, all the way into death.

John Waales was a practical man. He knew when it was time to quit, count your losses and gains, and move forward to the next adventure.

This should have been his last dig, his last adventure, and then back to the peace of his academic life at U.C. Berkeley, to sort all of this out and write a paper on his exploits in the Amazon. Given a second chance, he would never have come into this cursed mine again. But now, it was too late. His only hope was that word had gotten out to those people who would be concerned. But if the Chibchas were tired of him, then this could be their "golden opportunity" to get rid of him..

He thought about his two previous attempts to find the Lost El Dorado. It had been his obsession since he was young, and the reason he had become an archaeologist in the first place. His wife had died years ago, partly because of his obsession, and his daughter almost died last year because of what he had to do in the jungles of the Amazon.

Sitting there, he laughed wildly at the thought of his obsession. "My God," he thought, "I'm going mad."

Looking up at the walls, he suddenly heard the clanking again. It was coming from the other side of the cave-in, but more to the side. He looked at the wall and could see a small light coming from the left top of the wall, as though there was a crack in the rocks and light was coming through.

He looked at the cave-in. It was rough and rocky, approximately 15-20 feet high, but the slope was not as sheer as he had first thought. He looked for a way to ascend the cave-in and get up to the crack.

As he began to climb up the rocks slowly, he slipped a couple of times, but did not fall. He was about 7 feet off the ground and the rocks were stable, so he was able to get up another 5 feet easily. At 13 feet, he reached an impasse, as it was too sheer to go up. He was able to move to the left a few feet, which put him directly under the light.

It was easier to climb here, and the higher he climbed, the louder the clanking sound got.

He grabbed onto a large rock that was jutting out, and was able to hoist himself up the rest of the way. He could then lie on the rock and peer through the crack into the light. The clanking was loud and steady. There was air coming through, damp and musty, but better than the air in his own tunnel. He knew the river was nearby, but didn't know if he was next to it, or under it.

As his eyes adjusted to the light, what he saw made his blood run cold. At least a dozen Natives were at work digging, and tapping at the walls with picks, in a large cavern next to, and on the other side, of his tunnel. He had no idea who they were, but the way they dressed reminded him of the bad tribe of the Chibchas, who were under the order of Chief Omagua. Since this was a couple of miles away from the village, was it possible that a few of them had escaped and were mining gold on their own? Or was this a different tribe altogether?

He knew for certain it was not his hosts, the good Chibchas, because he would have known about this dig. In fact, he estimated they were on the opposite wall of the mother lode he had found, which had caused the cave-in when he tapped at it. They had to be close and, if they found him, they could easily kill him and no one would know. Since they were on the other side of the wall, it was only a matter of time before they discovered the gold wall that he had found.

John Waales slowly made his way down the rock cave-in. Once he reached the floor, he sat down to think. He turned his flashlights off, except for the tiny one he carried on his keychain. The other danger came from the river. He was fairly certain that both chambers were underneath the river. If the cave-in had weakened the outer walls, then there could be a second cave-in, this one with millions of tons of river water.

There had to be a way out of this. He looked back up at the light coming from the crack in the wall. They must have heard and felt the cave-in, but were probably grateful that it had not happened where they were digging. He was getting tired from lack of food and little to drink. He took a swig out of his canteen and decided to lie down on his back. He stared up at the light from the chamber, as though the Natives might crash through at any minute and attack him. In a few minutes, he drifted off to sleep.

CHAPTER SEVEN

THE VILLAGE OF THE LOST EL DORADO

THE PT BOAT HAD BEEN ROARING all night. They were less than a mile now from the Lost El Dorado village. They did not have the doctor with them, as they had been requested. Hopefully, he was already here and working to cure the young Prince Damien. Then they could focus on finding and rescuing John from the cave-in.

Jack was on the starboard gun, with Kimmi on the port gun. Manolo was out of bed now and, except for a good bruise on his forehead, did not look too much the worse for wear. He was on the Oerlikon cannon in the stern. Earlier, he had made some toasted egg-and-bacon sandwiches. The food was rough, but good and the crew consumed it quickly.

They were now on high alert. Bill, who was driving the boat, had told them that the Chibchas were tired of John being here, and wanted him gone. They were all surprised because they had helped the Tribe last year and they had told John he could stay and explore for up to three years.

John had made plans to get out of El Dorado with some gold as severance pay, but had this one last mine to finish exploring before it caved in. The Chibchas, had been doing everything they could to rescue John, but when they finally reached the cave-in, it was impossible to get through. They couldn't even try to get a secondary tunnel down because they thought the cave-in was at least a thousand feet wide, and ended, at the river.

Bill had been told that they estimated that John's cave was probably actually, under the river, down twenty feet or more below the surface. That would have been at the top of the tunnel. So, even if John was alive, they would not be able to pinpoint his location without ground-sensing sonar.

As Bill began to idle down the engines, he saw several Natives in boats, paddling toward the PT boat. He came to a stop in the water and held his position. The Natives, who were Chibchas and smiled and waved as they approached.

"Jack, Kimmi, take your hands off the weapons. Manolo, come up here and toss the rat line over into the water so they can board." Manolo went to the port side and threw the heavy rope line into the water. Two of the Natives came aboard. They smiled at Bill, and one even snapped off a crisp salute.

"Are you going to lead us in?" Bill asked the Native. "Yes," he smiled, showing his even, white teeth. "My job!" He proudly stood next to Bill on the bridge.

The second Native lay on his stomach on the bow of the boat, as Bill resumed going forward very slowly. The remaining Natives trailed behind in their canoes.

The Native on the bow was gesturing for them to move forward and then to the left, where what appeared to be the landing area on the shore. In another 50 yards, he indicated they should turn the boat left. While it appeared to be a solid riverbank, Bill knew this was actually the entrance to the river, which ran directly to the village. As he picked his way along carefully, the shore gave way to a mass of vines and shrubs that were easily driven through, and then fell back like a curtain after they passed through. The Natives in the boats behind simply moved the vines away as they passed through them.

"Any piranha?" asked Bill. The Native next to him shook his head.

"What about the doctor?"

"We brought him in yesterday."

"Is he having any luck?"

The Native shrugged and looked out at the water. As they rounded a bend, they could see the village. There was no dock, so Bill beached the boat by gently moving it next to the shore. The two Natives onboard the PT boat, each grabbed a line and jumped over into the water. They pulled on the boat so that it was next to the shore and tied it up to the trees, which lined the shore.

As they tied up, several more Natives came out and approached the boat. Both Jack and Kimmi secured their guns and climbed out of the gun turrets. Manolo was told by Bill to stay aboard and keep watch, as the rest of them jumped onto the shore and began to move out toward the village.

"Why aren't we going after Dad?" Kimmi asked Bill, obviously upset and worried about him.

"We have to make contact with Princess Cornelia and Chief Damien first," said Bill. "We need to ask about the baby, out of respect, and find out if the doctor they brought in has been able to help him."

"Then we need to ask what they have done to help John so far, and then make our plans from there," continued Bill.

Just then, a burly Native came up to them and announced, "Welcome to our village. The Princess wants to see you immediately."

Bill nodded his head slightly. "Please take us there at once. We are at your service, sir!"

The big Native nodded and, turning around, led them to one of the larger buildings near the river.

They entered and looked around.

The atmosphere was oppressive. Torches burned, illuminating the entryway, with shadows dancing across the gold ceilings. This was one of the original buildings made of gold, which was more ornate than functional. There was an entryway, two bedrooms and one bathroom, set up for the family who lived there.

Bill, Jack and Kimmi stood in the entryway. The Native bowed to them and exited through the front door.

After a few minutes of uncomfortable silence, Princess Cornelia, walked out through the door leading to the bedroom and looked at them without expression.

"I want you to see my baby," she said.

They walked into the back bedroom. A very small boy lay on his back on a very tiny bed. As they approached, he seemed lifeless.

Kimmi covered her mouth with her hands. Bill asked softly, "Is he dead?"

Princess Cornelia shook her head. "He is not dead. He is

undead. Someone has cursed my son, and put a spell on him, and he is about to die."

"Bullshit!" Bill burst out, before he had time to think.

Princess Cornelia regarded him carefully. "It is not 'Bullshit,' Captain Treese. My son's life hangs in the balance!"

"My apologies," said Bill. "So, what is happening?"

Princess Cornelia looked down sadly. "What is happening is that my son is dying, and no one can stop it." She started to cry, beside herself with grief.

"He's my son, damnit!" she wailed.

Bill went over to her and took her in his arms, where she sobbed uncontrollably.

The others looked uncomfortable, but didn't know what to do.

After a minute, Cornelia regained her composure. "Thank you," she said. "I am OK. I still have my other children, my husband, my brother. I love them all." She hesitated, "But no one knows what if it is like to be in fear for your child's life unless you have been through it."

She paused, "No one."

Jack asked, "Where is the doctor who was brought in to help your son."

Cornelia smiled. "We brought him here yesterday. He did everything he could. Set up an IV, giving him fluids. The drugs he brought, which should have revived my son, should have made him feel better and wake up."

She shook her head.

"Nothing helped. Nothing. He was almost worse when the doctor left than when he had arrived. The doctor said that he had some other ideas. But he was in a hurry. He said there was someone coming who was responsible. He kept grabbing his chest, as though he was in pain. He kept getting out of breath. The last thing he said was that she was coming for him. That he had interfered. That, his life was now in forfeit. He didn't care. He was going to help us no matter what.

"We didn't blame him. He was very upset that nothing he had tried had helped. He wanted to go into the jungle and search for native herbs and plants that might help my son. This morning, he didn't come back. We went looking for him. Down by the river, we found him."

"He was dead. No signs of a struggle, no blood, just his body lying face up, with his eyes and mouth wide open as though he was trying to scream for help. Trying to help the right people in the wrong place at the wrong time." She shivered and shook her head vigorously as if she was trying to erase the memory.

Cornelia crossed herself three times, and put her hands on her temples in anguish. "This is insane. My God. My son, my son, my son!" she wailed.

Bill continued to rock her gently. His Big-Bear arms holding a tiny mother who was in anguish.

He said softly, " Where is your husband, Mondo?"

She stopped her sobs and looked up at Bill. "I don't know. They were supposed to be here two days ago, but there is no word. Maybe these bad people have captured him. If he were here, he could help us, along with his dozen warriors. They are the elite. The best. Fish, fight or guard. They are our life. They will kill anyone who tries to hurt our people,"

Bill took a deep breath.

"Princess Cornelia, I will do my best for you. I don't know what to do. I'm not a doctor, and I don't know that Doctor Jack, here, can help your son. I do know that I need to try to get Professor John out of danger immediately, then, maybe he and I can help your son. But I don't know." His voice trailed off. He continued, "If I go to try to rescue my friend John from the cave-in, would you think I have abandoned your son?"

Cornelia looked into his eyes. "We have started to hate John, through no fault of him. We want to be independent without you two, but we don't hate you." She paused, "We just want to be left alone. You have helped us with that, but please understand, we want to be just the Chibchas now." She lowered her head and started to cry. "I'm sorry. I'm sorry."

Bill hugged her until she finally fell asleep in his arms, out of sheer exhaustion.

As he got up, her nurse came forward and helped lay her down on a straw cot.

The nurse looked at Bill, Kimmi and Jack. She reached out and grabbed Bill's arm. Squeezing it with force and with burning eyes she said, "You get them. You get them all and kill them. Bring our baby back to us."

She added, "You owe us!"

Bill, Jack and Kimmi all nodded. "You're right," said Bill. They headed back to make their plans.

Back at the boat, Bill pulled out a chart for that part of the river, in this case a tributary of the Amazon.

Bill spread the map out for Kimmi, Manolo and Jack.

"Here's where we are. Two miles upriver is where the entrance to the tunnel John went into. He descended into the tunnel, but we don't know how far. We think it was below the river, but we don't know where, exactly."

"We have ground-piercing sonar that can pin point John's location." Bill hesitated. "I'm going to say some things now that may be difficult to hear." He hesitated again and his voice grew louder. He began to pace around the small galley.

"Damnit. John is my friend and I know he is your dad and also your friend, Jack. But I care for him as much as anyone on this earth, and I don't want any arguments or bullshit when we go to rescue him."

"I know what I need to do to get him out. You can all have your opinions. You can be a mate, or a crewman, or even an officer. But once before, I let you know that I am the Captain, and we're going to do it my way. Again. Any questions?"

Kimmi was looking at Bill with eyes that were, although brimming with tears, fierce with determination. Jack nodded in agreement with Bill. "Let's get him out and go get those fuckers!" he said.

They cast off and headed upriver.

****

Charlie, Thomas and Zenadia, after having flown in the lead helicopter, landed at the airstrip, along with over a dozen mercenaries. It was really just a large area cut out of the jungle, around 500 feet in diameter, but it served its purpose. It was about 5 miles from the village.

The soldiers were all wearing jungle fatigues, boots and helmets. They were heavily armed, with machine guns, side arms, military-issue Ka-Bar knives, hand grenades and other incendiary devices. They also had the two stinger missiles, which worked on planes, as well as on any targets on either land or sea. It was early morning, and the jungle was already warm and humid. It was going to be hot. They were motivated to get this done quickly, with minimal loss of life on either side. The best scenario would be total surrender by the Natives, but nobody really believed that would happen.

Thomas was in the lead, dressed and outfitted like the soldiers. Charlie was in the back, also dressed for battle. Zenadia was behind her, without guns or any other protection. She was wearing her usual loincloth and a top made of leopard skin. Her hair cascaded wildly down her back. She walked freely, unlike the soldiers, who, like Thomas and Charlie, walked silently, in a crouched, combat position. Also, unlike the others, Zenadia was at home in the jungle and knew that nothing here could harm her. She could hear the sounds the others could not. She could also see deeper through the thick canopy than the others could.

When the soldiers saw Zenadia getting out of the airplane, they first looked at her young half-naked body with lust, but then, after a few minutes, somehow realized that she was dangerous - in a way they couldn't fathom. One by one, they touched the crosses or sacred religious medallions they each wore around their necks and would not look at her. Some said a silent prayer that, if any one of them was to die first, let it be her.

They had gone about a mile when Charlie looked back to check on Zenadia, but she wasn't there! Startled, Charlie stopped in her tracks. She looked around quickly, but there was no sign of her daughter. She realized that the group was beginning to get away from her, and she made the decision to move ahead quickly and continue to protect their backs. She knew that Zenadia could take care of herself. Her daughter was actually older than she looked and, as Charlie well knew, this jungle was her first home.

****

Zenadia ran through the jungle silently and effortlessly. She was going to find Bill Treese and his boat. She had already settled the score with the doctor who had come to save the baby, by reaching into his mind and his thoughts. He could see her eyes in his dreams and then in his nightmares. She waited until he was alone in the jungle looking for his useless herbs and berries trying to help the baby Prince Damien.

From halfway across the world, she revealed herself to him as he turned around at the sound of a tree root snapping - she had made that noise on purpose. The sight of her as a demon caused his heart to stop, as she had already weakened his heart by voodoo, once she knew who it was coming to try to help the baby.

She ran around the village, going on a tangent to find the boat upstream. No one could see or hear her. She reached the river, and saw the boat moving upstream slowly. It moved forward about a hundred yards, then turned around and moved back about the same distance.

She could see a younger man driving the boat; an older man and a young girl manned the two machine guns. Bill was nowhere to be seen. She squinted her eyes. It was still early morning, but it was getting lighter by the minute. Her eyes rolled back in her head, and her mind scanned the boat. She could see Bill in the radio chart house just below the bridge, headphones on, looking at a chart. He had a red pen in his hand, and was making dots on the chart.

She snapped back and looked out at the boat again. She made her plan and ran back to the group led by Thomas. She appeared behind her mother - who did not notice her reappearance. It was as though Zenadia had never left.

****

Bill was listening intently. The towed sonar buoy was getting signals from below the bottom of the river, but the problem was, there were too many signals. The ground-penetrating sonar was picking up too many life forms. Maybe, as many as 14 or 15 pings. He was also looking at heat tracers. Several were concentrated in one area, but there was one by itself approximately 100 feet away. From their position, they looked to be approximately 90 feet below them.

Treese yelled up to Manolo, "All stop!" Manolo stopped the forward progress and put the boat on auto so that the small motors fore, aft and on the sides would hold their position, to keep them from drifting.

"Should I drop anchor, *Capitán* Bill?"

"Negative. Just hold our position. We may need to move out in a hurry, and I don't want to have to pull up an anchor." A few minutes before, Bill had suddenly felt a sensation that he was being watched intently. Not the boat itself, or the others on deck, but him alone. He felt the hair on the back of his neck stand up, and he shivered in spite of the heat, made all the more intense by the cramped quarters of the chart house he was working in.

He came up on deck, and, grabbing his binoculars, scanned both sides of the shore, and up and down the river. Seeing nothing, he placed the binoculars back on their hanger next to the wheel.

Without the roar of the engines, it was eerily quiet. Even the jungle, which was usually notoriously loud with the cries of birds, monkeys and other animals, was silent. Just the splash of the current against the bow of the boat made a little noise.

"I think I found him," Bill said quietly.

"Really!" came a delighted cry from Kimmi.

"Wait a minute," Bill held up his hand. "Finding John is the relatively easy part. Getting to him is the problem. The Natives knew what mine he went into. They searched as far as they could, until they hit the cave-in. He is far beyond that point now. By my estimation he is around 90 feet below us."

Kimmi's shoulders slumped and Jack looked upset, as he spat into the water from the starboard gun turret.

Bill continued, "So that's the problem. Now, how do we get him out?"

The others looked at each other. Manolo volunteered, "I can free-dive a long way down and search for some type of opening."

Bill smiled, "Thank you Manolo. I already thought of that. Besides, we have scuba gear on board. But even if we were on the bottom, it will be tough to see down there, because the water is murky. Plus, how would we get to him? We can't dig, because the water would rush in and fill the tunnel and John would drown."

"There is one more problem," he added. "I also saw other heat markers down there. They were about a hundred feet from the first one. If I had to guess, I would say there are other people down there, but I don't know who they are. The one by himself is likely John, but the others….," his voice trailed off. "They may be friendly, or maybe not. So, what do we do with them if they are not friendly?"

Bill looked at the shore on both sides, looking for landmarks to mark their position. He still didn't like what he was feeling. Once he spotted his landmarks and triangulated their position, he went back to his navigation instruments. He had marked their global position electronically, so that he would have an electronic "footprint" of where they were, as well as a visual dead reckoning of where they needed to be, just in case they had to leave suddenly.

Jack spoke up. "Were you able to map out the river bottom? Any deep valleys or hills?"

"Yes, and no. I mapped out the floor, but no valleys or hills. Mostly flat and sandy. Probably a layer of rock, but not a totally thick rock. It is possible that the tunnel they discovered was either an ancient lava tube, or possibly a very old tributary to the river. I can't explain why it runs underneath the river. It seems to continue on beyond, and parallel to the river. I'm no geologist, but I've never seen anything like it." He shook his head, puzzled.

"Why not let me go down?" asked Jack. "I'm an expert diver, and I might be able to see something down there. You said he was about 90 feet below us. So, assuming the tunnel is at least 15 feet high and the river was," Jack hesitated, "how deep?"

"70 feet, more or less."

"So that means there is about 4 or 5 feet of sand, dirt, silt and rock between us. Is it possible to use a light explosive to get through the rock without flooding the tunnel completely?"

Bill rubbed his chin thoughtfully. "Any hole big enough to get a man through or two men would likely flood the tunnel in a matter of 1 or 2 minutes. Also, what about the others down there? They are separated from the one person, who we are assuming is John. What would they do if the tunnel flooded?

Bill continued. "If there are several men down there, and we know they are not from the good Chibchas, because they told us they could not get to John, then they must know another way in. It is not likely they are all trapped in there, because we would have heard about it from the tribe. My guess is they are another tribe looking for treasure down there and if it is John in the next chamber or tunnel, they do not know he is there. Or, at least, are not able to get to him."

Jack insisted, "I would still like to go down there and look around. Do you have double tanks?"

"Yes, and a pony side tank for emergency air. But you have to be careful how long you are down there. You could get the bends, and I don't have a hyperbaric chamber lying around. You could easily die."

"Hell, I knew that when I left the Bay Area. Can I go? Can you help me gear up?"

"What about the giant piranhas? Last time you went into the water to go skiing, you almost wound up as fish bait!"

Jack smiled, "Oh, those things. We wiped 'em all out the last time I was here!"

Bill looked away, sighing heavily.

Against his better judgment, and with alarm bells ringing off in his head, Bill reluctantly nodded yes.

Before his descent, Jack went into the cramped quarters of the chart house to take a look at the sonar, radar and thermal images. Bill pointed to a drawing he had made on a waterproof slate that

Jack would wear on his right arm, to help guide him underwater.

Bill pointed to what looked like parallel tunnels. "This is the place we think John is. Whoever it is, he or she is still alive. We have no idea about how much air is in there, a lot or a little. Either way, he or she needs to get out of there as soon as possible." He then pointed to the second tunnel, "This is where we are getting readings of multiple people. I have no idea who they are, or if they know someone is in the cave on the other side of the wall. They had to have heard the cave-in, but, for whatever reason, that hasn't impeded whatever they are doing in there."

"How do you know that?" asked Jack.

"If you look down their tunnel, bodies are moving along, likely going out to wherever their base camp is, back in the jungle."

"Why can't we beach, find the entrance to that tunnel and then go in? Sounds easier to me."

"There are a couple of problems with that, Jack. First, with the radar and sonar I have, I can only go back a few hundred feet, not enough to make it to the opening. Another problem is that the entrance is likely to be hidden to keep people out. Also, if the people down there are searching for gold, they probably won't take too kindly to us just showing up and saying, 'Hi. We are here to rescue our friend!' Might not go over so well."

"Lastly, if they cannot get to John because of the wall separating them from him, then we probably can't either. So, it all adds up to a big mess."

Jack nodded, "I see your point."

Bill continued, "I have a couple of things for you." He brought out a head strap, that was connected to what looked like a camera and a flashlight. You wear this on your head. Wherever you look, this 15,000 lumens canister dive light will light up the area for several hundred feet. It will also send us a live feed, which will go into our computer, so we can see on the monitor. I will be able to communicate with you through a special earpiece that you will also wear."

"Unfortunately, you won't be able to talk back to me because of the regulator in your mouth, but you can flip over the map I drew for you and write on it. Two more things. You will have a small portable sonar transmitter, that will lead you down to where you are directly over John. Don't know how we're going to get to him, but maybe there will be some type of miracle opening, like an upside-down vent or a lava tube. Who knows? The last thing is you are going to be tethered to the boat. If we need to move out in a hurry, I'll try to signal you. But the best bet is to unclip yourself from the boat, lie on the bottom for a while, and then come up slowly. Someone not so nice might be waiting for you up here." Jack nodded.

****

Thomas and his group were now roughly one mile from the village. They hid in the jungle, virtually blending in, so that any passing Chibcha tribesmen could not see them. They made their plans quietly.

Thomas, Charlie and Zenadia, along with two soldiers who had the stingers, would circumvent the village and go near the river, where Bill and the others were. They knew the boat was looking for John's position and so would be preoccupied, not paying attention to the shore.

The other soldiers were to wait here in the jungle until they heard from Thomas over the radio, then they would move into position on the outskirts of the village. Any Native willing to surrender would be treated fairly, tied up and left wherever he or she was until the rest could be gathered. Any resistance would be met with immediate death.

The secondary plan would happen if they heard a firefight up the river where Thomas and his group were going. In that case, if the Natives left the village and their forces were divided, they were to go in and capture or kill those who were left behind.

Zenadia had made it clear that she wanted Bill Treese alive, and not blown to bits with the stinger. Thomas had agreed to her plan, but he also said that the mission was the most important thing on his mind.

The five of them moved out to the right in a flank position, moving silently toward the river. It was almost 8:00 A.M., and it was getting hot.

****

Thirty minutes later, Jack had put all of his scuba gear on, including the twin tanks, plus extra air. He had on the intense light and camera for feedback on his head, two dive knives, the sonar/radar apparatus to help him locate John, the earpiece so he could hear Bill's feed, and the waterproof slate with the map of the two parallel tunnels. Jack was wearing his weight belt, buoyancy control vest device, scuba mask and fins.

He felt like an astronaut.

Bill had maneuvered the boat directly over the spot where they thought John was. They had not dropped anchor. Manolo was in the port gun turret and Kimmi was in the starboard. Jack was getting ready to drop over the side.

Thomas, Charlie, Zenadia and the two soldiers took up a position on the bank of the river. The PT boat was approximately 100 yards offshore. It was completely stopped in the water. Thomas had quietly made plans with his two soldiers to disable the PT boat so that it could not be used against them during the fight that was likely to take place. One soldier was to shoot the stern out, so that it would likely not kill them, but would force them to abandon ship and be their prisoners.

It was too perfect, with the PT boat sitting still. Plus, one of them was sitting on the stern deck with scuba gear on, and would never know what hit him, when the stinger missile was launched. Thomas looked at his soldier and nodded silently. Suddenly, the soldier raised his stinger and started to fire. Zenadia turned and screamed, "Nooooo!"

She lunged at the soldier and pushed the barrel of the missile launcher downward as it fired into the water. She then swung her left hand into his face, knocking him backwards fifteen feet into the trees. He grabbed his face in pain. The force of the blow had broken his nose.

"Zenadia!" screamed Charlie, as Thomas jumped at her and tried to grab her. But he was too slow and she held up her hand toward him. The gesture closed off his windpipe; he grabbed his throat and began chocking. With a motion of her hand, and without touching him, he was lifted five feet off the ground.

"Zenadia!" she screamed again, "Let him go!"

Zenadia held him in the air for several seconds and glared at him angrily. Then, wth a flick of her wrist, and without touching him, she threw Thomas ten feet through the air into a tree. He fell heavily to the ground. Zenadia pounced on top of him.

"I told you he was to stay alive!" Zenadia hissed. Thomas nodded weakly.

Suddenly thousands of rounds of machine gun bullets from the PT boat fired across them, mostly too high, as they were all lying on the ground. However, the other soldier caught two rounds in his left arm. He dropped backwards, wounded.

Zenadia was about to hit Thomas, which could have been fatal, but Charlie grabbed her arm.

"You've made your point!" she screamed at Zenadia. "Now two soldiers are down, and Thomas is hurt. The PT boat that we needed to disable is moving out, probably with Bill on it. Now what are we going to do?"

Zenadia looked at her mother with all the lights of Hell burning in her eyes.

"Don't worry about it!" she hissed at Charlie. Suddenly, Zenadia bolted towards the shore and, staying under the bullets, dove headfirst into the river.

Just as Jack was about to drop over the stern of the PT boat into the murky water, they suddenly heard and saw, from the shore on the right, the unmistakable sound and flash of a stinger missile. It should have hit them, but for some reason, the missile dove into the river before it hit the boat. They heard an explosion deep down in the river and a huge plumb of water shot up and covered the boat.

"Jack," Bill screamed, "Come up here! We have to get out now!" Jack managed to stand up awkwardly on the deck, as the boat started rocking violently.. He started to move forward, but suddenly took two steps back and, saluting Bill, jumped clear of the boat feet-first and began to swim downward into the crazy current caused by the missile.

Bill angrily shook his head and pushed the throttle forward. It took a minute for the boat to rev up. He sat there feeling helpless, as he was sure another stinger was about to find its mark and blow them out of the water.

CHAPTER EIGHT

JACK AND JOHN

JACK KNEW THIS WAS A one-in-a-million chance to make it, depending on where the stinger hit. If the missile hit anywhere near the two tunnels, there had to be an opening there now. Unfortunately, who knew what had happened to the people inside? He swam against the current. The light on his head and the illuminated sonar on his wrist told him he was going in the right direction.

Rocks, boulders and debris, were all around him, as the missile had done its damage. Jack dodged a large rock that flew past him. He was almost at the bottom. He pulled up and protected his head while more debris fell around him. He looked at the sonar screen, covered in sand and silt. He wiped it off and tried to clear his vision.

He looked at it and determined that there was only one blip and one heat bloom. It looked like the one that held John, but he couldn't be sure. There were no more blips. There were over a dozen people/heat blooms, in the other cave, but now they were gone. Whether they left, were obliterated or drowned Jack didn't know. He could only focus on the one person obviously left alive. One tunnel or both had to be flooding fast, and he still didn't have a way in.

Jack said a quick prayer. He went to where he saw a depression, probably where the missile had hit, but there was only rock, sand and other debris left over from the likely cave-in. He swam to his left along a ridge, but there was nothing that looked like an entrance. He reversed his route and swam to his right. If there had been an explosion, outwards, there might be a hole big enough for him to get through. Water might be pouring in there, depending on the size of the cavern; but if enough time had passed, or if the hole was big enough, the water might have equalized and there would be less of a torrent or flow going in and out.

Suddenly he saw an opening! It was jagged, but at least five feet across, likely from the blast outward. Jack immediately dove into the chamber, which was completely flooded. There were no signs of life in the murk, but by checking his illuminated sonar, he could see there was some type of life ahead of him. But how was he going to get there?

John Waales had been asleep in the dark when the missile hit the chamber next to him. The entire area shook, and rocks rained down all around him. He could feel the pressure of the water rushing into the chamber and could hear the screams of the men next door. He looked up and sure enough, the crack in the wall near the roof of his cavern had gotten bigger. He knew it was only a matter of time until his chamber flooded too.

John looked up toward the rock for a way out past the landslide, or possibly, for a pocket of air or just anyway, he could get out. There was nothing.

Water was now pulsing through the crack and dripping all around him. Instinctively, he began to climb up toward the crack, he figured that the higher he climbed, the longer he might live.

He reached the outcropping of the flat rock right next to the ceiling where he had stretched out before, and did so again. There seemed to be no other way out. He began to recite the Our Father prayer, while thinking about his daughter Kimmi.

Jack proceeded forward toward the heat bloom. He had gone down to the floor of the cavern, which showed the person was present, but not their location and not the level they were at. The chamber was at least 15-20 feet high. He could see nothing to give him John's position. Jack began to float up slowly, looking for any opening. The wall was not really too wide, but he had to scan it completely, which was no easy task in the heavy, murky water.

Jack glanced upward and immediately saw the opening in the rocks. Water appeared to be escaping into the next tunnel. He kicked his fins twice, then floated up to the opening and looked inside.

John realized that his life was almost over, and, like a man who knew he was about to die, he screamed beside himself. Raw emotion took over, and his screams turned to sobs as the water reached his neck and started to cover his face. He held his breath for as long as he could and then, drowning, he thrashed twice and started to pass out.

At that exact moment, Jack banged against the hole in the rocks. Using the powerful flashlight strapped to his head, he could see John immediately in front of him. He reached to his right side, grabbed his octopus, an extra regulator hanging by his side, and shoved it, his head and both his arms into the hole. With his left hand, he grabbed the back of John's head and with his right hand, he shoved the regulator into John's mouth. There was no response from John. Jack vigorously shook John's head back and forth. Sleepily John opened his eyes and instinctively sucked in air. They stayed that way for over a minute. John's eyes began to clear somewhat.

Jack kept holding out his first finger and thumb in the OK sign, to see if there was a response from John, who obviously had no idea who the hell Jack was. But he recognized that he had brought air to him and that was good. Finally, John, made a fist, his thumb pointing upwards. To him that meant he was OK, but to a diver like Jack, that meant he wanted to ascend to the surface from this hellhole. Which, as Jack thought with a mild touch of amusement, realized that's probably what he really wanted after all.

Jack shook his head. "No!" he shouted around his regulator. "Are you OK?"

John got it, but was still confused and nodded weakly. Slowly, his oxygen-starved brain was starting to come around. He looked into his rescuer's eyes and, as if in a dream, realized it was his friend Jack looking at him! He was still very confused, but brought his hand up, touched Jack's face through the mask, and smiled.

Jack knew they had to get to the surface for about a million and one reasons, not the least of which was that this was a damn dangerous place they were in, plus they were 90 feet below the surface and they could get the bends or nitrogen narcosis, which would make them confused and disoriented. Also, oh, and, by the way, the last thing he saw before descending was that they were under military attack from the shore with stinger missiles!

Since the hole was not big enough for both him and his tanks to get through, Jack loosened his belt which held his buoyancy control vest device. Leaving it on the other side of the hole, but keeping both of the regulators in their mouths, he slipped into John's chamber.

He used one of his dive knives to open up the hole in the rocks so that he could slip himself back into the first chamber; then he pulled John along with him. Since John did not have a weight belt on, he floated up, while Jack, wearing a weight belt, started to descend. Quickly, he grabbed his buoyancy vest, slipped it over his shoulders and fastened the belt. He grabbed John and pulled him close. He had to find the way out of the cavern and back to the outside or they would both die.

Inside the murky chamber, he was becoming disoriented.

He looked back and realized there was a line from the boat he was still tethered to, leading up towards the top of the tunnel. He had no idea how it was still in place, because Bill had told him to get back on board, but he jumped in the river anyway. The boat had moved away. It may have been pure luck, or a miracle from God, that he forgot to tie himself to the boat, although the line was still attached to his wet suit.

There was no time now to think about why, or how, but, Jack, holding on tightly to John, who was getting more energy, was clamping the Octopus regulator tightly in his teeth. Jack did not pull on the line, but simply followed it to the opening at the top of the cave, and out into the river.

Gaining their freedom from the rocks, John, with a sudden

burst of adrenaline, tried to make a break for the surface, which would have been a disaster. Jack grabbed him and forced him back down. He shook he head violently. "No, no!" he screamed around his regulator. "Slow down!"

John nodded, looking sheepish.

Jack checked his air supply. He had about 750 pounds of air left;, that would have to do. There was no way they could follow the dive tables, because John had been below sea level for too long, but without air, he would die anyway. The best they could do, would be to ascend very slowly. Whatever was happening on the surface would have to happen without them.

Jack added a tiny amount of air into his buoyancy device. They started to ascend slowly, with Jack stopping every 10 feet for five minutes to regulate the nitrogen in their blood.

****

Bill was starting to move out, but suddenly realized that he couldn't turn the wheel, which had become jammed. He had inadvertently turned toward the shore where the stinger had come from. As he began to go around in circles, he chopped the engines and allowed the boat to drift toward the shore.

"Manolo, Kimmi, keep your guns trained on the shore! You see anything move, shoot it!" They both nodded quickly, on high alert.

Zenadia hoisted herself out of the water and walked over to Thomas. His shooter was still lying on the ground. "Their boat is disabled. I tied down their rudder because I want them alive. If you can't figure out how to do it, I'll show you," she said.

Thomas nodded, "We were just supposed to blow off part of the rear, deck, not kill them."

"Did you know that Bill had extra fuel tanks installed by the stern deck? Your missile would have detonated it and destroyed them all!"

"How the hell did you know that?" asked Thomas incredulously. Zenada had never been aboard the PT boat, as far as he knew, while he had been held on it for over a week!

"Haven't you figured it out? I know things. You want to stay safe? Just do what I tell you to. You can command your toy soldiers, but Bill and his crew belong to me!" she said with deadly seriousness.

"OK, so now what?" Thomas asked.

"Their engines are off. Show them the missile, and tell them you will fire it on them unless they surrender immediately. Tell them to paddle in and surrender."

She looked at Thomas, "We need to head back to the village to make plans. Can you handle this?"

Thomas looked at her. "Yes," was his simple reply.

"Good. If not, you're a dead man."

****

Bill heard them call out from the shore and told his crew to stand down. Using his side and aft thrusters, he slowly moved the boat a few miles per hour into the shore. As the PT boat hit the soft sand, the two wounded, but still-functional soldiers, jumped aboard. They had their weapons out. Thomas appeared from behind the canopy of the shore.

"Hi, Bill! Good decision! Great to see you again!"

Bill looked at Thomas silently, and said nothing. This was merely a temporary setback, as far as Bill was concerned. He, Kimmi and Manolo were then bound up and led off the boat. They started walking back to the village at gunpoint without protest.

****

When Jack and John reached the surface over an hour later, Jack's tanks were completely depleted of air. In fact, he had to use his spare scuba Pony air tank to get them the last few feet to the surface. John, who was slowly gaining his strength back, wasn't feeling well at all. Jack looked around. There was no sign of the boat!

Jack knew that the shore to the right of them was the shore of the Chibchas, while the shore to the left was foreign. He started swimming with John to the right side. Halfway there, he spotted the PT boat beached onshore. He swam a little faster, remembering the giant piranha and their jaws of death. Reaching shore, Jack dragged John up onto the beach where they collapsed.

John lay on his back, drinking in the fresh air. Although it was hot and humid, it was like sweet nectar compared to the thin, dank air, that was in the cave. Jack stood up first, moved next to John and sat down. "Are you OK, John?"

John blinked twice. "Is there any water?" he asked hoarsely.

Jack got up slowly on weak legs. He shed all of his scuba gear onto the sand and moved towards the boat. It was obvious that no one was aboard, nor did the bad guys expect anyone to pop out of the middle of the river – otherwise, they would have left some sentries.

Jack climbed aboard. There was no sign of a struggle. *Odd*, he thought, because he knew Bill would rather give up his left nut than give up his boat. But there would be time to figure all that out later.

He went below and brought up a canteen of water and some dried apricots. It was something light for John that would have plenty of sugar and not upset his stomach.

Jack jumped off the boat and sat next to John, helping him sit up, and let him drink water slowly out of a cup. John coughed a few times but was able to keep the water down.

"How do you feel?" Jack asked.

John answered hoarsely, "Terrible. My back hurts, my legs aren't working right, I feel weak, tired and I'm a little dizzy. I also feel a little sick to my stomach."

"You're suffering from the decompression sickness, or, as it is commonly known, the bends. The dissolved nitrogen in your blood is coming out of solution and is forming gas bubbles in your circulation."

"Why do my legs feel so heavy?"

"That's all part of it. We did as many decompression stops as we could, given the air I had available. I think you will be OK, but uncomfortable for a while. If there was time, we would fly you to someplace that had a decompression chamber."

"Jack, why are you here? Why is Bill's boat here? Am I dreaming? The last thing I remember is drowning, in a cavern filled with water. Can you bring me up to speed, please? Oh, and as a side note, thank you for saving my life! I am sure that story will take a bit of time also."

Jack smiled. "Ok. I'm going to give you the short version, because a lot has happened in the past week."

"Thomas Reichen escaped his prison, and might be heading back here. On the journey to find you, we were attacked twice, once by two fighter planes and once by a submarine. Then, whoever was on shore just now shot at us with some kind of missile, but it missed! It went under the boat and hit the bottom!"

"I was just about to dive down to look at the bottom's layout. I was hoping there might be a way to reach you. Then, when we were attacked, Bill ordered me to get back onboard. But I jumped in the water instead! I thought the missile might have blown a hole in the tunnel - which it did. I checked my sonar/radar Bill had given me, and it indicated one life form down there, and I hoped it was you! There were over a dozen other life forms in the cave next to you, but they must have been killed by the ordinance, unless they were able to escape."

John nodded weakly, "They were mining on the other side of the wall you pulled me through. They were mining. You said 'we'. Who was on the boat with you?"

Jack took a deep breath. "Me, Bill, Manolo and," he hesitated, "Kimmi."

John rocked his head back and put his hands to his face, covering his eyes.

"Damnit! She is supposed to be in school, not in this God-forsaken place!" In spite of his passion, and because of his condition, the words came out weakly.

"John," Jack said, "she's the one that called me! You couldn't have kept her away with an army. She's your mamma bear.

Anyway, this was supposed to just be a rescue mission, not all of this insane fighting."

Jack hesitated again. "She's all right, that daughter of yours. She held her own, and saved our butts a couple of times."

"So where are they now?"

"I don't know. When I jumped in the water, we were under attack. Since the boat is not destroyed, and is on the shore, but they're not here, either they have been captured, or they went back to the village to get more help."

John looked around, as if expecting them to come strolling out of the jungle. "Well, why walk back to the village? Why not take the boat?"

"Maybe it's disabled, but not destroyed."

"What is going on with the Chibchas? This was going to be my last dig anyway, because they wanted me out."

"That's the other problem. Cornelia's son, Prince Damien, is very sick. He's not expected to live."

"What the hell?" said John. "He was a little sick when I left, but was sort of ok. What's wrong with him?"

"They don't know. We saw him earlier, and he looked lifeless. They had a local doctor who knew about exotic diseases come in to try and help the baby. He couldn't do anything, and Princess Cornelia even said the baby was worse after the doctor was there. He was then going into the jungle to look for plants and medicines, but he never returned.

"The next day they found him dead."

"Dead?," John said incredulously, "From what?"

"They don't know."

They were quiet for a minute.

Jack asked John, "What happened to you? What happened down there in the tunnel?"

For the first time, a light shown in John's eyes. He spoke up with strength in his voice, "Oh, man," he paused and looked around as though someone might be listening, "Jack, I found it! The mother lode! The true El Dorado of legend! I was deep in the tunnel. It was late, and I was going to leave and go back to the village. Then I spotted a rock that looked different. I tapped it out, and it was a huge nugget. Pure gold! 24 karatI I covered it up, as best as I can remember, then there was a loud rumbling and the lights went out."

"When I came to, the tunnel had collapsed and, the cave-in revealed a gigantic solid wall of gold. It looked like it was tons and tons of pure gold! That kind of ore, could turn the world value of gold on its ear overnight! It would be like the California Gold Rush of 1849. It would destroy the lives of the Chibchas and change their world forever!"

Jack was silent for a minute. "That's an amazing story. But it would take a miracle to get that gold out now."

John looked Jack in the eye. "I think it needs to stay there. I don't think I'm going to ever tell anyone. We need to keep this between us."

Jack nodded, "OK." He looked around and added, "Now we really need to find out what is going on. Someone is after us. Someone with deep pockets is trying to kill us. Two planes and a submarine do not come cheap, not to mention the lives that were lost. We need to make a plan to get back to the village." He took a deep breath, "I'm going to go onto the boat to see if she'll start. Wait here and rest."

John nodded and started to drift off. His last thoughts were of Kimmiko and how he had, once again, placed his daughter in danger.

CHAPTER NINE

THE FIGHT FOR THE VILLAGE

THOMAS' TROOPS WERE STATIONED just on the outskirts of the village. There were only a few villagers up at that time, walking around, making preparations for the day. Suddenly, they all heard the explosion, as the stinger missile exploded under water, shaking the ground underneath them. Then they heard the roar of the machine gun volley from the PT boat, as it fired back.

The village was immediately full of Natives running out of their homes. It had been peaceful for over a year, and they were not prepared for the noise and chaos of war. But suddenly, here it was again!

The mercenaries took advantage of this and burst into the village, firing their guns in the air. The Natives had been heading toward the river, and looked upstream toward the noise. So, when the soldiers behind them began firing their guns, they all turned around in surprise.

Fortunately, while the year with no fighting had dulled their reactions somewhat, it was also a blessing in disguise. Shocked into inaction, they didn't move, but raised their hands in surrender.

The mercenaries surrounded the Natives and forced them to move to the beach on the river, where they made them sit on the ground. The soldiers began to bind the Native's hands. For some, they used zip ties, and for others, they used ropes.

Meanwhile, several of the soldiers went from house to house, looking for more Natives. The ones they found, mostly sleeping after an all-night job of guard duty or working in the mines, surrendered peacefully and joined the others on the beach.

When they got to Cornelia's house, the soldiers confronted her, but she was standing over her baby sobbing. Her nurse stopped the soldiers from taking her away, explaining to them that the baby was not dead, but was dying.

She asked them to leave her alone. There was only one entrance to the house in the front, which was visible from the beach. In an extreme show of mercy, even the hardened Master of the Mercenary Guard, nodded in agreement, and told his Lieutenant to watch the door and to leave Princess Cornelia alone in her grief. They could expect no trouble from this mourning mother, no matter who she was, or what she meant to the tribe. They all knew Princess Cornelia, would be rendered useless in the face of her son's tragedy.

The soldiers did force her nurse to go to the beach, but left Cornelia alone with her baby. She leaned over the crib, collected Prince Damien into her arms, and collapsed onto her bed, holding him tightly and sobbing, as though her tears alone could bring him back to life.

Charlie and Zenadia had arrived just after the villagers were rounded up and stood apart from them.

Just then, Thomas, Bill, Manolo and Kimmi walked into the village. The two wounded guards were with them also. They were brought to the beach, and were seated with the rest of the tribe. They did not see either Charlie or Zenadia.

Thomas looked around. This was going to be easier than he had thought. "Where is the Princess?" he asked.

One of the soldiers spoke up, "She's with her baby in that house. She's not leaving. The kid is almost dead."

Charlie, listening carefully, looked over at Zenadia, who looked away. The others could not hear them talking.

Charlie leaned over and whispered to Zenadia, "Are you going to let the baby go?"

Zenadia was pensive, "Not yet. He's where I want him. Don't ask again!"

Charlie looked away, but didn't say anything. Her daughter was obviously in charge, and she realized that she should not interfere. She knew that Zenadia had changed out here and there would be no going back for her.

Thomas looked around and spoke up again, "Where's the Chief? Where is Chief Damien?"

The Chibchas being held prisoner looked around and started speaking amongst each other. No one had seen him since the night before. Their voices began to rise with hope.

"Knock it off! Knock it off!" shouted Thomas. He turned to his number one soldier, "Find that son of a bitch!"

The guard told two of his soldiers to go find him. They took off, going from house to house, and hut to hut looking for him. When they had searched all the homes, they started moving into the jungle, with their weapons drawn.

****

When Chief Damien woke up that morning it was very early. He was upset about his nephew, worried about his sister, and afraid for his tribe. The night before, he had made arrangements with four of his elite guards to take his wife and daughter away from their home to a safe village 20 miles away, deep in the jungle. They had family and friends there and they would be safe. Two guards would stay with them and the other two guards would return to the village, but were told to be careful.

What Damien had to do, they couldn't follow or be around. Damien had been told by the Shaman, that there were bad people coming to capture them. Also, that he had seen his brother-in-law, his sister's husband Prince Mondo, up the river many miles away. There were problems with their boat, and they could not get back. They had started hiking toward the village, unaware that the young prince was very near death, and that the village was probably going to be attacked sometime soon.

Damien had left before Thomas' people had arrived and taken over the village. Racing through the jungle, he heard guns firing behind him. He stopped. He had to make a hard choice. Return to the village and try to help, where he would likely be captured or killed, or run ahead, find Mondo and his Natives and bring them back to fight? He started running forward again, feeling like he was abandoning his people, but hopefully being able to help them in the end.

He ran as fast as he could for over two hours, stopping for

five minutes to rest, panting hard, bent over with his hands on his knees, and then ran again for another hour. Suddenly, ahead of him, he saw them coming. He burst through a grove of trees and almost knocked down his brother-in-law!

Prince Mondo grabbed him and pulled him close. He looked into Damien's eyes. "My brother! Why are you here? What is happening with our family, our village?"

Damien was beyond being out of breath, but he told Mondo as best as he could, what was happening, while he gasped for air.

"Your son, my nephew, is almost dead, my brother! He is holding on by a thread. A doctor was sent for, but he could not help your child, and then we found him, the doctor, dead in the jungle! The Shaman told me that bad men were coming to capture us! The professor John Waales is likely dead from a cave-in in the cave he was exploring! As I was leaving, I heard gunfire. The bad men are attacking our village. We are in danger, and so are our people!

"We must get back immediately!" said Chief Damien.

Mondo threw his head back in anguish. "My son, my son," he wailed, "Our child!" I must get to him!"

Mondo continued, "What of your daughter, my niece and your wife? Where are they?"

"I sent them away with my guards. They are safe."

Mondo took charge. He spoke rapidly to his men, who were true warriors. Like Chief Damien's men, they would kill to free their fellow Chibchas. "We are leaving and will get there quickly. Let us be swift, and help our people and my son!"

With a shout, the men, Mondo and Damien took off on the trail home.

****

Charlie said to one of Thomas' soldiers, "Bring that man over to us," pointing to Bill.

Two of the soldiers walked up to Bill, "Get on your feet and come with us."

Kimmi and Monolo started to protest, but Bill cut them off with a shake of his head.

Bill walked between them about 30 yards away from the others. Charlie and Zenadia were out of sight. They soldiers reached a spot on the sand and pushed Bill down on his knees. He didn't protest, preferring to play it close to the vest. The more frightened and vulnerable he looked, the more they would relax and not fear him.

Bill was facing the rising sun, so that when they came, he had no idea who they were. He saw two shapes approach him, who looked female. He turned his head to look at them and one of the soldiers pushed his head down into the sand. Bill didn't protest.

The two arrived in front of Bill.

Charlie spoke up first, "So, Bill, we meet again after all of these years."

Bill knew who it was immediately, and he also reasoned that the other woman was Charlie's daughter Zenadia.

"Who is it?" he asked feebly.

Charlie placed one of her combat boots on his left shoulder, as the soldier was still holding down his head.

"It's Charlie, your old Brother-in-Arms!"

Bill shook his head, as if in confusion. "Charley? Charley? Which Viet Cong unit are you from?"

Zenadia, who should have read what was happening better, lost her head in her hatred and fury of Bill.

She reached in front of the soldier, grabbed Bill's chin, and forced his face up to hers and then directly into the sun, "Charlie! Charlie! You dumb bastard! Charlie, who you betrayed in the jungles of Viet Nam and me, her daughter Zenadia, who you tried to throw out of a helicopter when I was just a baby! Now we've come to seek our revenge and kill you!"

She released Bill's chin and allowed his head to fall back onto the sand. He stayed silent, his mind racing. *There is always a way out*, he told himself, just as he had believed for the past 45 years.

Zenadia in her rage, started to kick him in his side with all of the fury she could muster, which could have killed him, but Charlie spun around and moved in front of her.

"We have a plan! Stick to the plan!" Charlie shouted at Zenadia.

Zenadia, shrieking, and shaking in anger, turned and walked away furiously.

Spinning around, she yelled to the nearest soldier, who was clearly frightened of this demon girl, "Tie him to the altar! Now!"

There were several gold altars on the beach, which had been used for sacrifices to the giant piranhas. The victims would be tied to the alter, which was shaped in a cross and, once released, would slide downhill on a steel track in the sand to the shore. Once it was near the water, the force of the descent would cause the altar to cartwheel and toss the victim into the water - and into the waiting jaws of the giant piranha. If the ropes didn't release on time, the victim was still held upside down under water, where he or she was eaten alive.

Bill was hoisted to his feet and led over to one of the altars. He was placed on his back onto the altar, his arms spread out to the side and was tied down by his arms and feet. He was still thinking about how he could break out of this in order to do what he needed to do; first save his crew and the Natives, and secondly, to save himself.

As far as exacting any revenge on Charlie and Zenadia, Bill had no such desires. Charlie had suffered being kicked out of the Service, that she didn't deserve because of his inaction, and he had done nothing to save Zenadia from falling out of the helicopter. He felt then that she was evil, and this realization had paralyzed him.

Charlie asked Zenadia, "What are you going to do with him? The giant piranhas are not here."

Zenadia glanced at her mother, "Don't worry about it."

Zenadia stared at the river and, dropping to her knees, looked up to the clouds.

"Appear! Appear! Appear!" she shouted.

Suddenly, the Natives nearest the water screamed and tried to pull themselves up beyond the sand, away from the river, as the water began to froth and churn. The giant piranhas, some 15 feet long or more, who had been away for a year, had come back. The Natives had tried so hard to forget them, but now they had reappeared, jumping out of the water and spinning madly in the churning froth!

The Chibchas strained against their bounds, lest they be tossed into the infernal jaws of these devils by their captors.

Bill looked out at the fish, but instead of panicking, steeled his mind to his possible fate. He began to concentrate on his rope bindings and tried to plan his escape.

Kimmi and Manolo, both tied with ropes, looked over at Bill, who was a hundred feet away and seemingly ready to be cast into the river. They looked at each other and also at the nearest soldiers, who seemed to be transfixed by the mad motions of the giant fish, whom they had only heard of in legend.

Kimmi and Manolo had small razor blades tied into small slips in their sleeves. Bill had showed them how to do that while they motored slowly into the shore, before they were captured. No one took notice that both of them had slipped into long sleeve cotton shirts, in spite of the heat. Since they were tied back-to-back, sitting on the sand, they both slowly began to saw silently at their rope binds.

Bill, coughing hard, as though in distress, turned his head to the left and spat sputum toward the nearest guard. The guard responded by slapping him in the face and cursing him in his native language. Bill, as though dazed and apologetic, turned his head the other way and coughed hard again. On his second hard cough, he spat his own small blade into his right hand, which he covered immediately.

He then started to cut his own ropes, slowly, with minimal hand movements, but if, the truth be known – only to Bill and his Parish Priest back in Chicago, every time one of those giant fish jumped out of the water, he cut faster. (And said another Our Father prayer.) Sweat poured off his brow. He either needed more time, or a little diversion.

Thomas came over to Charlie and Zenadia. "These Natives are not going anywhere. I don't know how you brought back these giant piranhas from hell, but they could work to our advantage.

The Natives are already talking about complete surrender. They don't want to die or go back. They are already telling some of my Native guards they are willing to help us. The Natives know that the baby Prince is dying and that his mother, the Princess, will be grief stricken. Also, Chief Damien, is nowhere to be found, and they think he has deserted them. All this has put fear in their hearts, and, also, Prince Mondo, the baby's father, will also be useless, in his mourning for his son.

"It is time for a little demonstration. If you are ready to sacrifice Bill Treese to the fish, now is the time to do it, to seal our fate."

Zenadia smiled. Finally, her revenge would be complete. This bastard, Bill will be dead in a matter of minutes.

Charlie was less sure. Her feelings for Bill were betraying her. Once you've slept with someone you cared about, your feelings are altered forever. No matter what had happened, there was still a small tiny spot in her heart for Bill Treese. He was a warrior, a friend, a lover, and a human being who cared about people, above and beyond war and its consequences. Charlie had tried to harden her heart. Because she loved Zenadia above all else, and her daughter, would not quit wanting Bill dead. Her daughter had become a force, which was, as she had proved over and over again, unstoppable.

Zenadia moved toward Bill, who immediately stopped cutting his ropes and hid his razor in his hand. "So, here we are!" she smiled, licking her lips, "I'm going to enjoy watching this."

Beyond the end of the rack that would propel Bill to his death, many of the fish jumped and frothed in the water. Several of the Natives screamed in fear, even though they were on the sand, away from the fish.

"The fish like fat old sailors, especially cowards who run in the face of battle."

Bill smiled, "I've been on a diet. Too bad for them."

"Like I said, I'm going to enjoy this."

"Get on with it, and be on your way." He looked away, while he pulled out the razor, and started to cut the rope on his right hand.

"If you feel that way!" Zenadia, with a shout, suddenly pulled the lever that released the altar, which had not been used in a year and was somewhat rusty. It began to slide slowly toward the river, right into the waiting jaws of the giant piranhas!

"Ha, ha! Die, Bill Treese!" she screamed.

She was so focused on Bill sliding on the altar toward the river, neither she nor anyone else saw Kimmi and Monolo escape from their bonds and start running toward the sliding altar. Reaching it, Manolo grabbed the altar, trying to stop its descent, which had been hindered by 12 months of rain, sun and neglect, Kimmi, who had grabbed a large stone, tried to shove it into the track, blocking its progress.. It worked, temporarily.

Zenadia, realizing what was happening, screamed at the soldiers, "Get them! Seize them! Kill them!"

The soldiers began to run down towards the altar. Suddenly, machine gun bullets rained down on them, cutting many of the soldiers to pieces. Then the Financier's troops burst through the jungle and started to attack Thomas' soldiers!

The Chibchas, bound and terrified on the beach, did everything they could to dodge the bullets, but several were hit anyway.

Charlie and Thomas dove for cover, but Zenadia, who was in her own world, momentarily lost her focus on Bill Treese. Suddenly, she saw Andres Rameriez behind the attacking soldiers. She screamed at the Financier and ran toward him.

Andres was not at the front of the attacking horde. Unlike Thomas and Charlie, he was a relative coward who thought more about his money, his investments and the little girls he liked to play with, than being brave. Running toward the fight, he tried to stay behind his soldiers, letting them be shot at; some were hit by Thomas' men. He could see the girl Zenadia near the beach, facing him. Her eyes burned with pure hate, as she started towards him.

But he was here, and he was ready for her.

Zenadia, charging fast, was seemingly doing the impossible, dodging bullets and sniper fire, and then jumping through the air to land directly on Andres, knocking him to the ground! Reaching up, he hit her in her face with his right fist, rolled on top of her and kept hitting her over and over!

She smiled at him, displaying ferocious pointy teeth, which had suddenly changed and she howled with laughter. Her eyes had turned a bright red. Soldiers on both sides stopped fighting for a brief moment and crossed themselves. That howl was from the devil himself!

Andres did not stop fighting, and grabbed her around the throat, trying to choke her. In a guttural tone straight from the grave, she said, "Now you belong to Lucifer, my Lord!"

She kicked her feet under his stomach and pushed hard upward. He was hurled over her head onto his back as he landed on the beach, twenty feet away. In spite of his age and bulk, he sat up and turned to face her, drawing out his gun.

Zenadia jumped up and ran towards him, baring her pointed teeth! She reached for him, but the Colt .45 round, fired by Andres, hit her squarely in the chest.

She staggered backwards. This couldn't be happening! She was immune to bullets, or any other form of human attack. But then she looked down at her chest. Black blood was pouring from the wound! She should be dead, but something was keeping her alive. *Did she need blood?* she asked herself, and then giggled. There was no pain, just a fear that she would not finish her quest.

She could not help herself and ran to Andres, who was trying to keep himself upright in the sand. She grabbed him and, in spite of her wounds, hoisted him up into the air. Impossibly, she held him high over her head, preparing to throw him into the river.

He outweighed her by over two hundred pounds, but it didn't matter.

"You're going to need some of your nice liquor and young whores to go with you on your long journey to Hell!" she screamed. "I'll see you there!"

Just then, he pulled out his Colt .45, again, aimed and shot her full in the chest again, striking her heart! Zenadia fell back, mortally wounded. Andres fell onto his knees in the sand.

Impossibly, jumping up and moving forward, she gathered all of her strength, and turned, reached out and grabbed Andres around his fat body. Twisting hard, she flung him far into the river and directly into the jaws of the waiting giant piranha fish, who tore him to bits in seconds. His screams echoed through the canyons.

Andres' troops were not sure what to do, with their leader

gone, but their second-in-command told them to attack the village
and retrieve the gold.

They stormed the village and shot more of Thomas' troops.
Realizing they were victorious, they took over – and, to celebrate,
fired their weapons into the air, thinking they were now done with
battle.

Bill, lying on the altar which was now stuck in the sand, had
cut himself free, but acted like he was still tied down. He wanted
to wait and see what was happening. Also, he had no idea who
these new players were. He knew the first bad guys were dead, but
what they were in for now, he did not know.

Zenadia, withering in the sand, knew she was dying. It was
only her fury that kept her alive. She had two gunshots in her
chest, and was barely breathing.

Charlie was also lying in the sand and wanted to help both
Zenadia and Bill, but, because of their new captors, did not dare
move.

Thomas was lying on his stomach, acting as if he was
dead. Once again, his plans had been thwarted by unforeseen
circumstances. He glanced around silently, looking for a way to
escape from here and get back to the helicopter.

The commander of the Financier's army, Caesar, gathered
his troops around him. He had decided there were just too many
people to deal with. They needed to clean the slate completely
and start dismantling the gold buildings.

It would not be the first time this had happened. They could
just wipe it all away. Kill everyone, and take the gold!

The commander smiled, but the smile did not touch his eyes
or his heart. Sometimes being a soldier meant you had to make

bad choices that you would never make in the real world, the sane world. But sometimes, certainly, in the world of war where everyone could be considered a casualty.

Caesar turned his back to the people on the beach and quietly told the soldiers, "Go ahead and kill them all."

The men looked at each other. They were human beings, after all, but also knew they were expected to follow orders.

They racked their weapons and moved toward the Natives and the others on the beach.

In a minute, it would all be over.

They aimed their weapons on the helpless Natives, who began yelling and cursing at their intended fate!

Just at that moment, Prince Mondo, Prince Damien, and their elite Native troops burst into the clearing and, using their Army M1's, began to fire on Caesar's troops.

The army of the Financier turned toward them and returned fire. Suddenly, the fight was man-to-man, and weapon-to-weapon. Although Mondo's native troops tried to overtake them, several were killed and wounded.

Mondo's men received the worst of it, but they didn't quit and continued to press forward.

Both Prince Mondo and Chief Damien were wounded, but fought on. It seemed that all would be lost.

Suddenly, military fire from twin .50 caliber machine guns rained down on the Financier's troops. Immediately, Bill, looking up from his position, on the altar of sacrifice, recognized the sound of his PT boat coming toward them from around the bend in the river.

Someone was opening up the twin fifties and it would not be

good for those who opposed them.

Jack Paris drove the boat, and John Waales fired the port side twin .50 caliber machine guns. Two of the Financier's soldiers died almost immediately, as the swiftness of the counter attack took them by surprise.

Several soldiers broke free and fired their rifles and machine guns at the PT boat. One pulled out a hand grenade and threw it onto the deck, landing near Jack on the bridge. Fortunately, the momentum carried the grenade across the deck and over the other side, where it landed in the water. The explosion rocked the PT boat and caused John to fire high in the air, over their heads. The boat began to list, and the smoke started to pour out of the starboard engine. Jack immediately shut that engine off and capped the fuel supply, lest they be blown to bits.

Bill threw his ropes aside, and grabbing both Kimmi and Manolo up into his powerful arms, ran down towards the river.

Jack saw Bill and juked the boat over towards them. The giant piranhas were everywhere, around and under the boat. He could feel them thumping madly against the boat, trying to capsize it. The boat was still listing, and that made it hard to steer. He knew they were taking on water, but he had to get to the shore.

Bullets from the remaining guards rained around the boat. Staying low, Bill ran alongside the boat, which Jack slowed down, even though it was now being hit with more frequency. Luckily, there was no one below deck, or they would have been killed or wounded.

Reaching the boat, Bill threw Kimmi and then Manolo up onto the deck. He was only ankle-deep in the water, but out of the corner of his eye, Bill saw a monster piranha charging at him, about to bite off his foot! In that instant, he leaped out of the water and, clinging to the deck of the boat, yanked his legs out of the water and curled his knees into his chest. Heaving with air, he pulled himself up onto the deck.

That's when he was shot.

One of the soldiers, firing an AK 47, was aiming at his back, but Bill was too quick, so he wound up shooting him through the back of his right leg. Bill screamed; the pain almost made him pass out, but he was too tough and too old a sailor to stop now. Both Manolo and Kimmi reached out and grabbed him, dragging him behind the steel protection of the bridge.

In spite of the pain, Bill yelled, "Jack, get us out of here. Manolo, see if you can fix that engine, but stay low, below the waterline, even if you have to crawl. Tell me what other damage there is."

"Are we going back downriver?" asked Jack.

"No, we're getting out of range, but I want to get back and help those people get their village back."

Kimmi screamed with joy at the sight of her father and, forgetting the danger they were all in, threw her arms around him in the turret of the machine gun. Sobbing, she would not let go of him. "I thought I had lost you! Oh, I thought I had lost you!" she said over and over again.

Gently, John pulled her hands away from his neck and, realizing they were out of range of the bullets, slowly climbed out of the gun turret. They then embraced on the deck as they both cried with happiness.

Jack asked Bill, who was lying on the deck in the bridge, holding his leg, "Are you all right?"

"Well the round passed through my leg but didn't hit the bone. It just hurts like hell," Bill replied. He was starting to get light-headed and was afraid he would go into shock.

Jack lashed down the wheel and throttled down the two remaining engines. The river was wider here, so he could afford to get a little off-course. The piranhas were behind them now, showing more interest in the tasty Natives, who were still tied up on the beach near the water.

Jack went below and came back up with a tourniquet, hydrogen peroxide, an antibiotic salve and bandages. He put the tourniquet on Bill's leg and began cleaning the wounds and pouring the peroxide on them, one wound was on the front and one was on the back of his right leg. Jack applied the cream liberally and began to wrap Bill's leg up tightly. He took off the tourniquet. When he was done, he handed Bill two painkillers and a canteen of water. Bill accepted it all gratefully.

"Nice field dressing, Jack! I could have used you in my unit in Viet Nam!"

"I was in high school then!" giggled Jack. "I was on the golf team, and trying to lose my virginity!"

They both laughed. Bill got to his feet, keeping most of his weight on his left leg.

"Manolo, what's the damage down there?" Bill called down through the open hatch on the bridge.

Manolo came up on deck, soaking wet.

"*Capitán*, there is a hole and a leak in the side just above the waterline, but when the boat moves, it lowers and takes on water. The engine has some damage, but I can fix it if we can pump the water out. But we have to be careful it does not blow up! There are a lot of bullet holes in the sides, which also leak. There is about a foot of water throughout. I started the bilge pumps fore and aft and they are working. When do we have to go back? The monster fish are going to attack, and there are still the soldiers to deal with. And why were the first soldiers attacked by the second soldiers? I don't understand."

Bill nodded, "You are right, little *Amigo*. The first soldiers were led by Thomas Reichen, who had taken us as prisoners. I don't know who the other mercs were, unless they were sent by someone to steal whatever Thomas took. Let him do the dirty work, and then go in and take the spoils!"

"Whatever, let's put a Band-Aid on this boat and get back into the fight!"

Manolo nodded and went back below deck to continue doing repairs.

"John," said Bill, "it's good to see you! I won't ask what happened, or how you and Jack came to drive my boat, but your timing was excellent!"

Kimmi nodded in agreement.

John smiled weakly. "I'll give you a full report when I'm able. I'm still pretty sick. Since it is wet down below, can I lie down in the day cabin for a few minutes until we go back?"

Bill nodded yes, "Kimmi, can you tend to him?"

She nodded and helped her dad into the day cabin, which was just aft of the bridge. Because it was right above the fuel tanks and in front of the engines, it was usually pretty hot in there. But John had to get out of the sun.

"What's wrong with him?" Bill asked Jack.

"He has the bends, and maybe a little nitrogen narcosis. His blood is not good and he's confused from the nitrogen in his blood. I went all the way to the bottom of the riverbed, found a hole in the top of the tunnel next to him, swam down, found another opening at the top of the tunnel leading into his tunnel and found him! He was submerged and barely alive until I stuck that regulator in his mouth and slapped him around a little to make him breathe."

"Then we had to get out on limited air. Since he had been below sea level for who-knows-how-long, I had to make decompression stops every 10 feet for five minutes. Never even came close to the dive tables, which would indicate a safe ascent. So, he has the bends, and we don't have a decompression chamber, unless you picked one up while I was gone."

Bill shook his head sadly. "Nope. We need to end this thing as quickly as possible and get him down river for some medical treatment." He smiled at Jack, "Nice work by the way. That was an incredibly dangerous and stupid thing you did, but I'll forgive you this time because you both made it back alive!"

Jack smiled weakly. "If I ever have to pray that hard again, I would hate to think of what kind of predicament I had now gotten myself into!"

Bill nodded. He took over the throttle, easing himself onto the bridge captain's chair, while being cautious of his wounded leg.

They moved out and began to make their plans.

****

Back on shore, Charlie hugged and hovered over Zenadia, who was on her back and breathing very shallowly. She was moving in and out of consciousness. She had lost a lot of blood, but something or someone was keeping her alive, at least for now.

Lying a few feet away, Thomas realized he would not be able to survive this unless he recruited the new mercenaries and got to the helicopter. Slowly, he got up. One of the guards sprang at him at once, holding up his AK 47 automatic rifle. Thomas spoke in rapid local-dialect Spanish to him. The soldier nodded, and backed away. He went to his Commanding Officer and whispered something to him. The CO grunted and walked over to Thomas.

"I am Caesar," he said. "And I am now in charge. Andres is dead. What are you proposing?"

"That PT boat is still out there, and their goal will be to liberate the village from us or, actually from you. You and your men are great soldiers, but you have had many casualties. Your men bested my men, that is true, but we both have the same objective."

"And what is that?" asked Caesar.

"The gold. It is here all around us. More than we can spend in a lifetime!"

"So why do we need you? We have the gold, and the Natives are our prisoners. That boat may be fierce, but she is wounded and running on only two engines. Plus, we have put many holes in her, and she may be sinking."

"You are right," said Thomas, "and you would be out of this, except for the boat's skipper."

"Who is that?"

"Bill Treese."

Caesar put his hand to his forehead, "Ah, I know of this man. He is clearly a dangerous *hombré*. His deeds live up and down this river. What do you propose? We have the gold. We will not run.

We can set an ambush for his return."

"No, we need to take the fight to him. We came in on our helicopter gunboat that is not far from here. We can gather up your men, leave everyone here bound, and fly back and attack the boat with our weapons. We still have one stinger missile left. Once in the air, we attack!"

The Commanding Officer thought about what he said. He was right, they only had himself and seven soldiers left, plus two of them had minor wounds and could not survive a direct assault or even hand-to-hand combat. Plus, if these Natives were freed, they would join forces to save their village. So, he made the decision to trust Thomas.

"*Adelanté*! Let's be on our way! Caesar whistled to his soldiers, who fell in line and raced out of the village.

CHAPTER TEN

THE FINAL FIGHT

ON THE BEACH, THE VILLAGERS saw the soldiers running into the jungle and did not know what to think. They called out to Chief Damien and to Prince Mondo, who were both wounded by the fighting, but they were lying unconscious, near each other, just behind the first row of huts.

Hearing the shouts from their tribesmen, they both woke up, regained their feet and moved forward cautiously. Damien had been shot in the fleshy part of his left arm, which hurt more than it was serious. Mondo had many cuts over his face and arms, and had also been hit on the back of the head with the butt of a rifle.

Looking into the clearing, they did not see any soldiers, nor did they see Bill Treese, or the girl or the boy who had helped Bill. Their fellow tribesmen shouted that they were gone, and that they wanted to be released.

Damien said, "Go to your wife and son, brother. I will release our fellow brothers and cousins." He rushed forward and began to cut them all loose. Unfortunately, there were some casualties, as many had been caught in the crossfire.

Prince Mondo ran into his home to be with his wife and dying son.

Chief Damien asked his people what had happened, but they didn't know. Several who had been released, began cutting the ropes and ties binding the others.

He asked those who had been released, to help care for the wounded and get them off the beach. The Natives who had died, sadly, he couldn't help.

Chief Damien looked back at the jungle with a worried expression on his face as though he knew they would return, but he didn't know how.

****

Thomas, Caesar and the soldiers sprinted back to the clearing in the jungle where the two helicopters were waiting. There was no sign of the pilots.

Caesar and the others called for them, but there was no answer. Thomas grabbed Caesar, and said, "Don't worry, I can fly this thing! We only need one. It'll carry all of us!"

Caesar nodded and yelled for his troops to climb aboard. One had been carrying the stinger missile they brought, and the others all had fully automatic AK 47's. Plus, they had hand grenades. The Sikorsky UH-60 Black Hawk had been outfitted with external machine guns, but for some reason, there was no ammo. So, they knew they had to use light arms and the stinger to destroy the PT boat.

Strapping himself into the pilot's seat, Thomas began pressing buttons and throwing levers. The motor roared to life, and within minutes they were in the air, heading for battle.

****

The PT boat was not 100 percent, even after the repairs had been made. Manolo cautioned Bill against using too much speed too quickly. They were heading back to the village, preparing to repel boarders.

Bill was at the helm, Jack on the starboard twin .50 calibers facing the occupied shore, Manolo on the port twin .50 caliber. Kimmi was in the day cabin, tending to her dad. At a moment's notice, however, she could run out the back and man the Oerlikon cannon on the stern of the boat.

Bill tested out the engines and found that all three were working, but the boat was handling somewhat sluggishly. Below deck, there was still a lot of water, which was being pumped out madly by the two bilge pumps.

Manolo had also patched the large hole in the side, which had been damaged, first by the hand grenade, and then by the relentless pounding of the piranhas.

They first saw the helicopter right in front of them. Rising above the jungle canopy, it looked like a speck, way off in the distance over the river, and came at them from the front. Bill knew immediately this was a problem, even at over three miles away, he saw it was a warship.

"Battle stations," he said quietly, but above the roar of the engines. He threw the switch, and the familiar sound of "General

Quarters" rang out.

Jack and Manolo brought their guns around to face the incoming invaders, who were closing in fast.

"Can we shoot?" asked Jack.

"Do not fire unless fired upon," was Bill's terse reply.

They didn't have to wait long, as the gunners on both sides of the open hatchways began firing a volley of light arms machine gun fire on the approaching PT boat.

They ducked down as they passed underneath the Sikorsky Black Hawk. Both Jack and Manolo pointed their guns upward and fired, even as it slipped through their tracer fire.

Bill plowed on, trying to get to the village to see what was happening there. He did not know who was in the helicopter, or even if the village had already been wiped out.

Suddenly, to make matters worse, the giant piranhas appeared out of nowhere and began to launch themselves furiously at the boat. Manolo had a bead on the underbelly of the helicopter, but just as he aimed, the boat was knocked sideways by the force of the giant fish, and he missed badly.

As Bill charged upriver, the helicopter spun around and followed them. He could see several soldiers leaning out and firing from the open hatchways. Bill juked the boat, turning left and right, faster, slower. He had done this in Viet Nam and also on the rivers of South America. He sped up and reached the village, roaring past it; but he saw no one on the shore. The Natives were either free, captured or dead, and he did not want to speculate which.

Suddenly, the helicopter, which was now chasing the PT boat, opened up with short bursts of very precise fire. Bullets hit the stern, the day cabin, the bridge and up through the bow. Bill ducked for cover.

"Jack, Manolo, can those bastards!" he shouted. Jack and Manolo tried, but the water was too rough and the piranhas, which had incredible speed, were still hitting them.

Bill turned the boat first right, then left, trying to come around to face them, where he knew he had a better chance. But it was no use. The Black Hawk had more speed, was more maneuverable and could climb above the surface and deliver a bomb or a missile.

In fact, it was just about to do that very thing. Thomas yelled for them to bring the stinger up to the open hatch and prepare to fire. A soldier leaned out the window, but he could not get an angle on the boat.

He yelled to Caesar, the Commanding Officer, that he could not get a clear shot.

"OK," yelled Thomas, "I'll get you a clear shot!" He started to climb and passed over the PT boat. Both war ships continued to fire at each other, with the PT boat getting the worst of it. Kimmi screamed as the day cabin was lit up, and her father was almost hit.

Kimmi burst through the front door of the day cabin, onto the bridge, and yelled at Bill, not realizing the seriousness of the situation.

Bill knew they were in desperate straits. He also knew they were going to launch a stinger at him, because they had pointed it directly at him and his crew when they were first captured.

Instinctively, he turned to Kimmi.

"Stay with your dad. Stay away from the rear gun. There is no use. If we are hit, get him to shore and to the Chibchas.

She nodded and immediately went back to the day cabin and her dad. Because of the volley of fire, Bill looked back, to see smoke pouring out of his engines. He knew he did not have much time left.

He pressed the throttle and the boat shot forward as if from a slingshot. The move caught Thomas, who was flying the helicopter, by surprise. He jumped the helicopter up, noticing the smoke billowing from the engines of the PT boat, and smiled. This was going to be the best part - killing Bill and his crew! Briefly, he thought back to when Bill had him as his prisoner and Bill had the audacity to ask him if he was "In Country," referring to Viet Nam. Thomas knew more about espionage work in Southeast Asia, than Bill could have ever dreamed of.

Thomas smirked, "*Pussy Navy frog,*" he thought.

Thomas passed overhead, while his men continued firing into the PT boat, which was again taking on water and becoming sluggish.

"*All the better,*" thought Thomas, who shot upstream and banked his helicopter around until he was over the water by 20 feet. He hovered there as Bill's now crippled boat was heading upstream toward them, coughing and billowing smoke.

Thomas yelled back, "Get ready with that stinger. I'm going to enjoy watching this!"

One of his men came forward and, lying on his stomach, pointed the stinger out of the port side of the helicopter.

"Kimmi," Bill yelled, "I need you now!"

She ran out of the day cabin. "What? Dad's hurt. I need to be with him!"

Quickly came Bill's reply. "Grab that flare box at my feet. And don't argue!"

She did it.

"Take out the flare gun and train it at the helicopter we are approaching. Don't do anything until I tell you to. But once I tell you to fire, you have to shoot it, or we will all be dead."

Kimmi panicked, "What if my aim is bad?!" she yelled.

"Just shoot in the direction of the helicopter. The Stinger will take care of the rest!"

She steeled herself, knowing this was life-or-death. She reached into the box, and grabbed the large flare pistol and held it up, aiming directly at the helicopter ahead of them.

Suddenly there was a puff of smoke from the side of the helicopter, as the stinger missile was launched. The helicopter was still over a quarter-mile away but was approaching fast.

"Now, now, now!" screamed Bill, as Kimmi pulled the trigger and the flare shot out toward the helicopter and started to move upward.

In an instant, the missile intercepted the flair and there was a gigantic explosion, which rocked the PT boat and spun the helicopter around.

"You sonofabitch!" screamed Thomas. "OK, this is personal!" He launched the helicopter up to over 1,000 feet, then turned back towards the PT boat came down with all the speed and fury he could muster. Over one mile upstream, he could see the PT boat in front of him.

Bill saw Thomas' maneuver and was ready for it. He pushed all three of his throttles forward, going at 100 percent of what he had left on the engines toward the helicopter.

Thomas revved his throttle forward and now, only 10 feet off the surface of the river, charged Bill's PT boat head-on!

As the helicopter closed at over 100 miles per hour, Caesar, in the passenger seat, screamed out; but Thomas, his face set in stone, was determined to finish this.

Meanwhile, Thomas' soldiers continued to fire on the approaching PT boat, which was taking on more heavy casualties. Automatic fire penetrated the boat into the bow and across the sides. More and more water was entering the PT boat, threatening to sink it!

It didn't matter. Bill pushed the throttle forward as far as it would go, and kept it there. Jack and Manolo kept returning fire on the approaching helicopter, which was still approaching at 10 feet above the water. The exchange of bullets was reaching a crescendo and something had to give!

Jack yelled at Bill, who had a maniacal look on his face. "Are you insane?!"

Bill looked over at him. The boat and the helicopter were on a collision course, which would be over in less than 20 seconds.

"Only a few men and women in the world are willing to play chicken to the end to make the ultimate sacrifice. What do you think about this adventure Jack?!"

He grinned and howled with laughter. "Watch this!" he screamed.

They had closed to within 750 yards and Thomas suddenly became convinced that Bill would never back off. The C.O. Caesar, had moved back to the open hatch and was raising his weapon, in this case, a handheld Gatling gun, which he had already trained on the approaching PT boat.

"Swing me around," he screamed.

Thomas, immediately slowed the helicopter, pulled it to the right and exposed his port side to the PT boat, which was now only 200 yards away and closing fast. The landing skids of the helicopter were now touching the water, as they hovered, Thomas trying to keep the aircraft stable.

Caesar smiled as he started to squeeze the trigger of the Gatling-style Mini-launch-gun, a NATO six-barrel rotary machine gun, with a rate of fire of up to 6,000 rounds-per-minute, which would kill them all almost immediately.

Bill, his eyes rolling back into his head, went back into his mind, countering, countering, to time this situation precisely, pressed the button, firing the starboard torpedo, which had armed immediately, and was less than four seconds away from the hovering helicopter.

Thomas saw this, immediately and tried to pull up and away - but it was too late. The torpedo was on top of the boat in less than three seconds, striking the landing skids. The last thing Bill saw was Thomas Reichen, his eyes wide open, realizing he was finally in a situation where he was dead and done.

There was a gigantic explosion of the helicopter! Bill's boat, under its own reduced power, but still flying forward, did its best to get away. The fireball from the helicopter shot upward and all around them, as the intense heat threatened to consume them!

Parts of the helicopter rained down, and several fiery pieces hit the PT boat. Bill juked the engines, trying to move the boat away, and shut down both the starboard and port engines before they exploded, leaving the center engine to get them back to the village.

It didn't matter. Even though they were all unhurt, the PT

boat was done. Listing left and right, it was taking on water and would sink any minute.

Giant piranhas circled the boat, knowing they would soon be fed.

Bill gathered everyone, except John, who was still lying on a cot in the day cabin, on the bridge. "It is not done," he said. "The fish want us, and we are sinking. I would suggest we get on the weapons and try to kill as many of the fish as possible."

They didn't need any encouragement, as Jack, Manolo and Kimmi, scrambling into position on the guns, opened up and tried to kill the fish, who, sensing their ultimate victory, tried to jump on the bow of the boat to sink her.

Bill was almost out of power. Even the center engine was giving out and they were about to be adrift. They were near the village, but no one was there. As the boat drifted and sank more, the piranha became more and more bold, banging into the hull and trying to jump onto the stern.

Kimmi screamed as a piranha launched itself out of the water and tried to bite her face. Now the boat had sunk almost to the deck and several of the fish were on the bow and others dropping into the stern. The boat was going down. Bill, on the bridge, grabbed his Winchester rifle, and spinning around, with water dancing around his ankles, used his gun to rapid-fire over and over, just by pumping the handle, like the "Rifleman" TV show of the 1950s. Several fish slid off the deck, dead, but many more jumped up to take their place.

It seemed to be all over, as the boat began to sink further, and the crew was at the mercy of the giant piranha.

Suddenly, hundreds of rifle rounds from the shore were heard

- as the Chibchas, began firing their M1 rifles at the giant fish. Several more fish, who were wounded, rolled off the deck and, either floated or sank to the bottom, where they died or were consumed by the other piranhas, who were cannibals.

The barrage continued, as Bill, Manolo and Jack sank down below their armored enclosures. Kimmi, diving back into the day house, covered her dad from the gunfire. He was wet from the flooding, and feeling worse by the minute. Finally, after several minutes, the fish disappeared as their dead kin floated to the surface of the river. At that point, the Natives stopped shooting, but stayed on the beach, watching intently in case more piranhas returned.

Bill, his engines dead and his boat sinking, used his side propellers, for the second time that day, to propel the PT boat into the shore, where the friendly Natives could finally pick them up.

For the moment, they relaxed. But only for a moment.

The Amazon River did that to you, they all thought.

By then, Bill had landed his PT boat on the shore, which had been virtually sunk. Only the deck was still out of the water. Bill ran back into the day cabin and helped Kimmi get her dad to his feet.

"Let's get the hell out of here, John," he said.

John didn't need any encouragement, as he let himself be pulled up and outside the day cabin onto the deck.

Bill, John, Kimmi and Manolo stepped off the boat onto the shore. They made their way to the village, and collapsed onto the sandy beach.

CHAPTER ELEVEN

THE EXORCISM

THE FIGHTING HAD FINALLY STOPPED, The Natives had killed the deadly piranhas and helped bring the crew off the PT boat, which was almost completely sunk. Prince Mondo had been inside his house, to be with his beloved wife Cornelia, who was holding their now lifeless son and weeping over him, as only a mother could.

He gently picked them both up and brought them outside into the sun. He wanted everyone to see what the real cost of allowing these foreign, American devils into their lives had cost them. They sat down in front of the house, Cornelia still holding the tiny, lifeless Prince Damien. With burning eyes, Prince Mondo looked out at all of them, both his tribe and the Americans. He was ready to kill to avenge his son!

"Look at what you have all done!" he screamed, and began to weep, in spite of himself.

****

Charlie touched Zenadia's cheek tenderly. Now that she was so helpless and vulnerable, Charlie's love for her knew no bounds. Tears started falling down from her cheeks, and landed on Zenadia's forehead. Her eyes suddenly flew open.

"I have to get to the baby," she whispered hoarsely.

Zenadia got up slowly and began crawling toward the House of Cornelia. Charlie was afraid to interfere and cowered on the ground.

Mondo, in spite of his anguish, saw Zenadia crawling towards them. He knew instinctively who she was, and that she was coming there to finish off his son, even though he was already, apparently, dead. Mondo would have none of this. He leapt up and grabbed his ceremonial sword, still sharp and deadly, off of the porch, where it was lying since the battle. He was going to kill Zenadia once and for all! He ran toward her, raised his sword high above his head, and prepared to deliver the final strike that would send her straight back to Hell, where she came from.

Chief Damien saw this and jumped up. With a flying leap, he tackled Mondo, sending his sword flying. Mondo started cursing him in their native language and reached for his sword. Damien leapt on top of Mondo and held him down.

"No, my brother!" Damien yelled at Mondo. "Leave her!"

"Bastards!" screamed Mondo, looking around wildly, "I will kill you all!"

By then, Zenadia had reached Cornelia and the infant Prince Damien. She raised herself up on her knees and asked to hold him. Cornelia, confused and not really knowing what she was doing, handed the baby to her.

Zenadia held the little Prince in her arms. She touched Prince Damien's head, and chanted. But this chant was different from the others. High and sweet, it sounded more like musical chimes rather than the guttural utterances she had made many times before. She made the sign of the cross on his forehead and handed him back to Cornelia, who was staring at Zenadia in disbelief. She had no idea who this girl was or where she had come from.

Cornelia looked down at her baby, who was now staring back at her, his eyes wide open. Suddenly he started crying, softly at first and then with gusto, finally ending with sobs as Cornelia held him, not believing what she was seeing and hearing. She started to cry as Mondo pushed away his brother-in-law, Chief Damien, and dashed toward them. Realizing that his son was alive and well, he put his arms around his wife and child, and then he too broke down, sobbing, but with relief this time.

A joyous shout went up from the Natives! Chief Damien jumped up and shouted for joy. Their world was being restored, even though they could not believe it.

While everyone was focused on the happy parents, no one noticed that Zenadia had started to crawl across the sand and into the river.

Bill, lying on the sand, was the first to see her. He jumped up, the pain in his leg now almost unbearable, and ran to stop her. He grabbed her and held her tight, yelling at Charlie and Kimmiko to keep her here. Zenadia was almost dead from the gunshot wounds, and would be gone soon. He called for Manolo, who also jumped up and ran over to them.

Bill looked into Manolo's eyes, knowing he might be sending

him to his death if there were still piranhas alive, and spoke to
him.

"Little brother," Bill said, "you have to run to the boat, grab
the vial of water on my desk in my quarters, and get back here
immediately. The vial is very heavy and is attached to the desk by
a line. You will have to swim in the dark, and there may still be fish
still in the water. Please be careful!"

Manolo nodded his head, yes, assuring Bill he would be
careful.

"I don't care, *Capitán* Bill. I will do it now!"

He sprang into action, jumping into the sinking boat, and
went directly to the chart house, which led below. As he sloshed
through the water, he knew immediately what Bill wanted. He
held his breath and, climbing down the ladder, which was fully
under water, he then swam into Bill's Captain's Cabin and, more
by feel than vision, retrieved the corked vial. He swam back up to
the deck, scrambled over the side, then ran toward Bill and the
others with the large vial of water.

Bill looked down at Zenadia, whose eyes had rolled back in her
head. She was not making a sound. "This is going to hurt," Bill
tells her. Bill then took off his Saint Michael the Archangel's gold
medallion, which he had worn around his neck since childhood,
and put it against her chest. She started to scream!

He pulled aside her shirt and exposed her now-heaving chest,
where the bullets had penetrated her. He poured the Holy Water
brought by Manolo into the two holes that had wounded her, and
they began to smoke and burn. She screamed again as the water
burned and bubbled furiously, penetrating deep into her body. Her
back arched, almost impossibly, as her feet walked backwards, all

the way to her head. She held that position for almost a minute, as though straining against invisible ropes.

After one last scream, she passed out, her body going completely limp, while still lying on her back. The wounds, burning internally, sealed themselves with a huge scar, as the smoke began to clear.

Suddenly, everyone holding her was flung backwards away from her body, with a scream and a force not of this earth. A shadow, dark and shapeless, rose from her body and hovered over her, screaming silently, but so that everyone there could see it and hear it.

The Natives closed their eyes and looked away as it jumped up and spun away into the jungle with a violent explosion, which leveled twenty of the surrounding trees. It flew away, across the river screaming.

On the ground Zenadia tried to sit up but couldn't. She looked at Bill and Charlie, who were next to each other lying on the sand. They both crawled to her side.

"Zenadia," said Bill, "stay still. We can save you."

"You already did that," came her weak reply. Then she passed out again.

"Is she dead?" Charlie asked, tears already forming in her eyes and dropping down her cheeks.

Bill looked down at her, "Not anymore," he said, "Saint Michael the Archangel triumphs over Satan once again, with God's love and for the sake of Jesus Christ!"

Zenadia's mask of fury was gone. The evil hatred and clenched teeth were gone. Even though she was much older, she now looked like a teenager sleeping contentedly after a happy prom dance. There was nothing but a peaceful expression on her face.

"Jack," Bill motioned for him to come over, "can you check her?" he asked.

Jack felt her neck for a pulse, which was there, but very weak. He pulled back her eyelid; her pupil was large and dilated, but contracted visibly with the light.

He leaned over the ugly scars on her chest and listened to her heart, which beat rapidly, but unevenly. He could not tell if it was fibrillating or just irregular, and missing a few beats on and off.

He looked at Bill and Charlie, "I think she will be OK, but it seems she is in shock. Maybe we can put her on a bed, under some blankets and keep an eye on her."

Prince Mondo and Cornelia had been watching and listening to what was going on. He whispered to his wife, who nodded silently.

Prince Mondo stood up. "Doctor, please bring her to our hut. We will place her in a bed and watch over her." He looked over at his wife's nurse, who was still lying on the beach a few yards away, and nodded to her. She sprang into action, as Bill picked up Zenadia and carried her into the house of gold, followed by Charlie and Jack.

After a few minutes, Bill and Jack returned to the clearing.

Prince Mondo was still hugging his wife and son, who had also been set free from his imprisonment. The baby was looking from mom to dad, and started crying for food. He was hungry. One of the tribesmen, an assistant to the Prince and the Princess, realizing this, jumped up and ran into their dwelling to get food for the baby.

Chief Damien stepped forward and, against protocol, embraced the Americans.

"Because of you, we are now truly free!" he said, as he hugged them all again.

"What do you ask of us, and what can we give you?" he continued.

Bill was upfront. "Your Highness, I need nothing more than some time to fix my broken boat and then I will leave you, possibly for the last time, unless you need something from me. Then I will return posthaste." He smiled, as Damien nodded silently.

Chief Damien moved to Professor John Waales, who looked like Hell and obviously needed medical attention as soon as possible.

"Doctor Waales, what can we do for you?" he asked. John shook his head. "I am done here," he said weakly. " You have been most gracious, but my work is finished and you need to heal your village without me, or anyone else from the outside. Thank you for everything, my friend."

Chief Damien smiled. "I understand. Heal yourself also, my friend." He bowed to John.

Charlie walked out of Chief Damien's nephew's home.

"And what of me, Chief? I am responsible for much of this. And what of my daughter, who lies sick in your care?"

Chief Damien thought for a minute. "She will stay, as this is where she belongs. The demons have left her, and we will train her to be what she was meant to be, a South American Indian. You are permitted to leave. But," he continued, "if you are ever compelled to return, you will be killed. That is the price you pay for your life and your actions."

Charlie bowed her head respectfully. "You have your nephew back. Your sister has her son back. What of me? Zenadia is my daughter. Why can she not leave with me?"

"That is the price you pay for your wickedness. She belongs here, not with you in the U.S. However, if she should ask to return to you, be assured we will find a way. Of course, if we feel you are a danger to us in the future, we will kill you both."

Charlie looked away and smiled briefly, as if in disbelief.

Damien continued, "Our small reach even extends to the community of Blackhawk in your small town of Danville, California."

Charlie snapped her head around and looked at him.

"Never underestimate the powers of your opponent," Damien stated. "Evil will be paid back by evil, and kindness will be paid back by kindness. Your choice." It was a veiled threat, which should not have had to be uttered. But, Damien knew that sometimes people will surprise you, especially if they do underestimate you. So sometimes the threat must be presented to avoid further bloodshed.

He smiled. "You are free to go. There is one helicopter left, and you can fly it. I know that. It will take you to the jet you arrived here on. We know that also. Jack, Kimmiko and John will accompany you. You will take the Professor to a hospital to save his life, as he is now dying."

"Bill and Manolo will stay here to fix their boat for one month, maybe less, maybe more. Then we will be done with you. Don't ever come back. Our borders are now closed to the white man."

"Bless you," Damien added, looking at all of them. "*Vaya con Dios!*"

Charlie nodded respectfully.

Damien disappeared into his sister's house to check on

Zenadia. Prince Mondo and Princess Cornelia followed, carrying Prince Damien.

"Hey, Chief Damien," called out Jack.

Damien reappeared, "What is it?" he asked.

Jack continued, "Uh, It's kind of late, and I know we need to leave with John as soon as possible," he hesitated.

"Yes, Jack?" asked Damien.

"Uh, is there anything to eat? I hate to ask, but we're all starved."

Prince Damien stared at Jack. He lowered his eyes and smiled.

"I'm sorry doctor. What would you like to eat?"

Jack looked toward the river at all the dead giant piranhas. "Filet-O-Fish?" he asked hopefully.

Chief Damien smiled. "Yes doctor, can we pack you a lunch? Is that OK?"

Jack smiled, "That would be excellent, Chief!"

As they waited for their food and prepared to leave, Kimmiko and Manolo walked hand-in-hand toward the beach, away from everyone. They sat down on the sand. Across from them was the mostly submerged PT boat. They looked out at it, ever mindful of any stray piranha fish lurking about.

At first, they didn't say anything, and just sat silently. Finally, Kimmi said, "I guess it's goodbye again Manolo. We never seem to catch a break, do we?" She sniffed, starting to cry in spite of her toughness, and looked down at the sand.

Manolo smiled. He reached out and turned her face toward him. He then leaned over and kissed her gently on the lips. "We did get a break Kimmi. Your dad, Jack and my Bill are alive. But you have to get your dad to a doctor and get him well. *Capitán*

Bill and I will get the boat put back together and leave this place forever. You told me you only have a year left to study. I will wait for you to come back here, if you will have me."

"Do you mean it?" she asked. "There are lots of girls down here in the Amazon Basin," she said as she looked up into his eyes.

He smiled and hugged her tight, "Yes, but there is only one Kimmi."

They both fell back on the sand and kissed passionately. They held each other tightly, until it was time for her to go.

****

Bill walked over to a still-shaken Charlie. "Hi Charlie," he said in a friendly tone.

She looked sideways at him, still in pain at the sudden loss of her daughter. "There is nothing I have to say to you, Bill Treese. You have totally fucked up my life and I want nothing to do with you!"

"Uh, can we walk down to the beach for a second? There are a couple of things I have been waiting almost three decades to say to you."

Charlie sighed, looked down at the ground, and said "OK," as they walked down the beach towards the same gold altar Bill had almost been sacrificed on earlier.

She turned and looked at him, her face marked with fury.

"OK. Here we are."

Bill had this great speech all planned, and was ready to deliver it as soon as he was able to. Ever the tough Navy man, now he was suddenly vulnerable and at a loss for words.

"Uh, uh," he stammered. "Uh, you are still really mad at me." He stopped and looked around as if searching for the right words, but there weren't any.

Charlie looked at him and shook her head. "Still a man of few words."

Bill looked at her. "I'm sorry," he said. "I am sorry about everything that happened. That day in the jungle in Viet Nam, you saved all of us, including me. I told that to my C.O. and do you know what he said? 'Shut up. It never happened.' The only thing they acknowledged, was that we got the soldiers out. The kids were never there. The V.C. blew up the hills around the village, not us or you."

"No one wanted to admit to a battle that never existed, over a border that was not supposed to be fought over."

"This belongs to you, and I have waited a really long time to deliver it to you. If you give it back, then it will be thrown into the drink with the fishes."

"What is it?" asked Charlie.

Bill reached out to her with his right fist closed. He held his hand out to her and looked her in the eye.

Charlie reached out her open hand.

Bill dropped his Navy Silver Star Medal into her hand. Charlie looked at it for a minute and tried to give it back to Bill.

"No! I don't want this," she hissed.

Bill stepped immediately in front of her, pressed his hand onto hers and closed it in her fist.

"Yes," he said. "This has been yours since that day In Country, when you saved all of us.

"It's not mine. It never was. Now you can keep it, or you can throw it into the river if you want to. But," and he paused, "if there ever was a courageous sailor, oops!" he paused," a courageous airman, it was you on that day! So please think about that for a minute. Your country didn't thank you, but I am."

Bill stepped back and snapped her a smart salute, "Thank you, Captain, for saving my life and the life of my crew, the soldiers and the children."

Charlie sighed. Years of angst and bitterness started to fall slowly away from her at that moment. She returned the salute, smiled and looked at the Silver Star for Valor.

"It's kind of pretty," she sighed. "Medals for lives, I'll never understand, but thank you. I will treasure it."

She paused for a long time. "I will always treasure you, too, Bill. Thank you."

The moment was becoming awkward, so they both embraced. Bill started to return to his submerged boat, and Charlie was returning back to the others who would be leaving with her on the flight.

Suddenly, she spun around., "Hey Bill Treese," she called out, "why don't you look up a lady and call her sometime?"

Bill turned and smiled. "Sounds like a plan to me! Are you listed in the phone book?"

"Jeez, Bill, what's a phone book? Just Google me!"

"Uh, OK. How do you spell 'Google'?"

They both laughed, and she shook her head.

"See ya later, Bill Treese!"

CHAPTER TWELVE

THE RETURN HOME

CHARLIE, JACK, JOHN, AND KIMMI made it through the jungle, with an escort from Chief Damien's guards, to the helicopter pad. Charlie was able to fly them back to the Bogota Airport, where the same people met them as before. After a brief discussion, they decided to leave John and Kimmiko in Bogota. He needed medical care, and probably at least a week in a hyperbaric chamber.

Once the plane left the Bogota Airport with Charlie at the helm and Jack in the back, the darkness enveloped them once again. Jack, feeling somewhat lonely and isolated, grabbed two lime-flavored mineral waters from the galley and came forward into the cockpit.

"Hi," he said to Charlie, "need a water?"

Charlie, her face illuminated by the instrument lights in the darkness of the cockpit, had been focusing on her take-off and on setting her flight plan toward San Francisco Airport. She smiled gratefully.

"Thank you, Jack."

Jack sat in the right seat in the cockpit. Instinctively, he strapped himself in. They were silent for a long time.

Finally, Jack asked, "So, are you OK?"

Charlie stared straight ahead.

"I don't want to talk about it."

Jack smiled, "Me, neither. But if you did want to talk about it, what would you say?"

"What are you? A fucking psychologist?" Charlie said angrily, turning to look at him.

"No. A few Master's Degree Courses in Clinical Psych, at Cal State Hayward, but nothing that qualifies me as a shrink. Some say as a chiropractor, I'm more of a stretch than a shrink!"

They were silent for a second.

"But it seemed there was a lot going on between you and Bill, who is my friend, and also your daughter Zenadia, who was left behind. It also seems you are upset, so I just want to help. Is that OK?"

Charlie sighed, "It's a really long story."

Jack smiled. "It seems we have a lot of time until we get to SF."

Charlie looked resigned. She took several deep breaths. She had seldom thought about it, because it hurt too much and she had never spoken to anyone about that day. "OK, it all started in Viet Nam."

After two hours, Jack said, "Wow! That's a hell of a story. You know, Bill told me some of it. He also told me he never got over the fact that, you got shafted by the military, and that, in fact, you were the hero who that saved them all that day. He gets a medal, and you get kicked out of the Service. You and I both know Bill is a true warrior, who lives and dies for his troops, not for himself."

Charlie looked down and nodded.

"Yes, but he didn't do much for Zenadia."

"True. That's something he has to answer for, and I think he has."

They were silent for a while.

Jack said, "If you get tired, let me know. I have a private pilot's license myself!"

"Really?. What are you typed in?"

"Uh, Cessnas. 172, I think."

Charlie smiled, "Jets?"

"No."

"Instrument-rated?"

"No"

"Multi-engine prop, even?"

"Uh, no." Jack smiled sheepishly. 'Is that important?"

"It's OK, Jack, I got this!"

They both smiled.

"You know, Jack," Charlie sighed with resignation. "I already miss my daughter. And those bastards back there think I am done," Charlie looked out at the darkness fiercely.

"Charlie," Jack started, "without making any judgments, and with all due respect, you both did not come down here with the best of intentions."

She looked sharply at Jack, who continued, "We've all been through a lot. Let it rest for a while. I'll bet she calls you in a few months and wants to come home."

"Why would you say that, Jack?"

"She's changed, and wasn't it Arthur Fields who said, 'How ya gonna keep 'em down on the farm after they've seen *Paree*?'"

Charlie smiled and bowed her head. "Thanks, Jack, I hope you are right."

****

Two weeks later, John and Kimmiko caught a commercial flight back to San Francisco Airport. John was mostly healed and, with the exception of a few headaches and still the heavy feeling in his legs, he felt better than he had in weeks.

Jack met them there. After that, they drove back to the East Bay and went to their favorite pizza hangout at the top of Solano Avenue in Albany.

After two deep-dish pies and several Anchor Steam beers, Jack asked John the obvious question, "So, are we done?"

Ruefully, John rubbed his chin.

"Yes. We are done. The Chibchas made it clear that we were done with the region and the exploration. They graciously thanked us for our help in reuniting the village, and then graciously told us we were not welcome any more, and we were advised to never visit there again."

John smiled.

"We should have left there after the last time. What the hell," he said, as he lifted a large slice of combo pizza to his lips and knocked it back with a slug of Anchor Steam beer from the tap.

Jack and Kimmiko both smiled and looked at each other.

Kimmi spoke first, "So, Dad, Uncle Bill said he had a line on a deep hole in the ocean off the continent of Brazil, with a ton of ancient artifacts inside. Are you going there?" she asked sweetly.

Professor John Waales, in spite of his training and trying to maintain a strict poker face, turned to her and said enthusiastically, "Hell yes!!!"

THE END

EPILOGUE

IT WAS AFTER MIDNIGHT, almost two months later. Charlie had long gone to bed, but her cell phone on her nightstand was going off.

She rolled over and answered it sleepily, not really paying attention to who might be calling her. It was a bad habit. She had gotten a little lazy lately. Maybe it was anger, maybe it was resentment.

"Hello?"

"Hi, Mom. I'm ready to come home," was Zenadia's reply.

Charlie shot up in bed, adrenaline flooding her body.

"How, honey?"

"Bill is taking me to Bogota, and I'm catching a plane back home to you."

Charlie swallowed hard, "We'll both have a lot to talk about. Will it be OK?"

"Yes."

"I want us to be good, " Zenadia added.

"OK, love you," Charlie said.

"Ya. Me too."

Charlie set the phone down and wept.

www.ingramcontent.com/pod-product-compliance
Lightning Source LLC
Chambersburg PA
CBHW070019120726
47909CB00003B/993